DOWN AND O

# DOWN AND OUT IN BEVERLY HILLS

A Novel by Ian Marter
Based on the motion picture from Touchstone Films
in association with Silver Screen II
Produced and Directed by Paul Mazursky
Screenplay by Paul Mazursky and Leon Capetanos

A STAR BOOK
*published by*
the Paperback Division of
W. H. Allen & Co. PLC

A Star Book
Published in 1986
by the Paperback Division of
W. H. Allen & Co. PLC
44 Hill Street, London W1X 8LB

Phototypeset by Input Typesetting Ltd, London
Printed in Great Britain by
Hunt Barnard Printing Ltd, Aylesbury, Bucks

ISBN 0 352 31863 5

# CHAPTER 1

Santa Claus beamed out of the clear blue sky, his swollen red cheeks – like the bulging buttocks of some huge Rubens Amazon – bursting with grotesque promise and abundant good cheer. In the early morning Californian light, the frothy white smoke of his beard hung like a solitary cloud stranded in the billowing sunrise of his red fur-lined costume. Behind him the glittering sleigh was heaped with brilliantly colourful parcels of all shapes and sizes, pouring gorgeously forth from the tinsely sacks of gifts. In front of him a dozen or so reindeer streamed ahead, their legs flying forwards and backwards like a Wells Fargo stage team running the gauntlet through ambush territory. Their Disney faces bore human smiles, reflecting the hearty spirits of their master as they raced in a perpetually freeze-frame leap across Wilshire Boulevard suspended between the streetlights. At regular intervals above the wide traffic lanes, identical Santas leaped in reckless merriment from one side to the other forming a magical tunnel of sparkling cheefulness with the other half-finished decorations slung from pole to pole and from one luxuriant palm to the next.

The sidewalks beneath were still mostly deserted, except for the odd liveried hotel doorman in braided cap and white gloves looking much like another species of seasonal decoration under the awnings, and for a few streetcorner newspaper sellers and a handful of muncipal workmen on ladders and crane-hoists busy rigging strings of lights among the trees. Here and there, janitors watered hanging baskets of flowers with long-necked watering cans in anticipation of brilliant sunshine ahead, and deliverymen made their morning rounds to restaurants, hotels and stores. But the traffic was already busy as business-suited men checked out of hotels and swept off in limousines towards the airport or downtown and as people began driving down from the hills and in from the suburbs for the day's work.

Above the smooth hush of the gleaming limousines and the warm rustle of the wind off the Pacific, a dog could be heard yapping incessantly. One of the hard-hatted workmen who was wearing a *Dump Reagan* teeshirt glanced down from the cradle of the crane-hoist underneath Santa Claus's bulging crimson stomach and cursed at the racket. Below him, a filthy ragged figure with matted sandy coloured hair and a morass of beard was shuffling erratically along the sidewalk pushing a squeaking grocery cart loaded to the brim with personal flotsam and assorted garbage. The tramp was peering suspiciously up from beneath furrowed brows at the grinning rosy-cheeked cutout soaring merrily overhead. Sitting on top of the heap of bundles, newspapers, tins and bottles in the battered wire trolley was a small brown mongrel with tiny collapsed ears and tiny beady black eyes. Its tail was lashing viciously from side to side and it snarled with wild-eyed and bare-toothed savagery at the innocent workmen overhead.

The tramp paused to scratch his ass through the stained and ragged check pants resembling baggy clown's trousers that were hanging in smelly folds around his legs. 'Hey easy, Kerouac! Those goddam Beverly Hills reindeer might just decide to piss all over us.'

Up in the cradle, the workman glanced at the hammer he was holding and then back at the dog. The tramp seized the twisted plastic handle of the grocery cart with a muffled curse and shuffled quickly away along the wide sidewalk under the stirring palms. The workman looked up at the jovial plywood patriarch of seasonal goodwill with his snowy beard and cargo of goodies and spat very accurately into the jolly old man's eye.

Up among the luxurious secluded residences of Beverly Hills, David Whiteman came to in his massive white bed with the remote channel selector still clasped in his hand. As his eyes unstuck themselves and gradually revealed the white chrome and glass world, they focused eventually on the screen of the master-bedroom TV. With dumb joviality, Santa Claus shot from nowhere towards the viewers and swooped round and round above a model of a little snow-covered town – all church steeples and bright yellow windows – drawn by his rampant grinning reindeer. Suddenly his face zoomed in and filled the screen. His mouth gaped in a great belch of laughter and vomited forth a stream of toys – action men, computers, laser guns, A Team puppets, Cabbage Patch Kids, Little Nurse sets . . . David Whiteman groaned and rulled his hair which was already standing up like a field of short grey grass. He tweaked his neat grey moustache and yawned. Santa Claus shot back into the horizon and the little town gave way to three inane females in Jane Fonda strip doing simpering aerobics.

He glanced across at the comatose figure lying on the other side of the vast bed. Barbara Whiteman lay on her back, her eyes covered by a black sleeping mask decorated with little silver leaves. Her brightly lipsticked mouth had dropped open slightly, but no snores emerged from her full, sensuous lips. Her breasts, like Santa's cheeks, rose and fell with ample grandeur under the silk sheet.

With a sigh of resignation, David dropped the channel selector next to his wife's hand. 'Twenty years . . .' he muttered, easing his stocky body off the bed.

Instantly the long-haired bedside rug exploded into a storm of banshee wailing.

'Shut up, Matisse!' David hissed, struggling to keep his balance as he tripped over Barbara's highly strung black and white collie lying buried in the rug.

From the luxurious bed, his wife uttered a pathetic moan as if it were her that had been accidentally trodden on. David shot her a panicky glance as if willing her not to wake and tottered out of the huge white-carpeted bedroom.

On his way to the kitchen he came across a note addressed to him in his son's spidery handwriting. Puckering his sleepy eyes, he managed to read it without his reading glasses. With a sigh he screwed it up into a ball and wandered reluctantly into the vast living-room. Pulling a chair up to the video machine in its elaborate laser-disc stereo audio cassette and video cabinet, he punched the play button and stared gloomily at the screen. A frown of doom folded his slightly fleshy Paul Newman lookalike features as Max Whiteman appeared gazing intently into the camera.

Max was a handsome sixteen year old with a punkish hairstyle dyed a violent red straggling spikily over his shoulders. In one ear he wore a gold ring. 'Hallo Dad, I just want you to know why I'm being so silent lately,' he began, with a disarmingly frank and shy smile. 'It's nothing personal Dad . . . It's just that I feel it's impossible to express what I'm feeling in words right now. So here is a tape which expresses my state of mind . . .'

The screen went blank and David groaned and reached for a large cushion which he hugged like a child with its comforter. Then the screen suddenly lit up with naked teenagers on a beach: girls lolled in the sun, their brown bodies lightly covered with sand; blond surfers hung ten and did press-ups on their boards; Arabs appeared in flowing robes and sunglasses, holding strings with colourful kites flying in the blue sky; a huge frog leaped across a bed of water lilies; Santa Claus leaped across a boulevard in a blaze of lights; car wrecks intercut with gunfight clips from TV shows; a naked girl running across the sand in slow motion, her breasts moving in all impossible directions at once . . .

After thirty frantic seconds the screen dissolved into a snowstorm of static.

David sat staring at the screen, hugging the cushion and swaying gently from side to side. His blue eyes were baffled, but he was nodding slowly. 'The new Coppola . . .' he murmured. 'My son Max. Max the film maker.' He switched off the machine and gazed around him at the slightly vulgar *nouveau riche* decor, the paintings, the sculptures and the sumptuous furnishings, the gilt fittings and glass tables.

'Mad Max,' he sighed, tossing the cushion aside and wandering out and into the bathroom.

The main bathroom of the Whiteman residence was a magnificent affair. Spacious enough for a family of ten, it was tiled and mirrored and equipped with opulent extravagance. It contained not only a bathtub, a shower, a lavatory and a *bidet*, but also a giant jacuzzi with a control panel resembling something out of the Space Shuttle.

David stared at himself in the mirrors. Today he looked fifty five rather than approaching fifty. His face had grown heavier and his belly was in danger of overtaking his chest. Feeling decidedly under the weather, he opened the mirror-fronted medicine cabinet and contemplated the orderly ranks of bottles, packs and phials without enthusiasm. David hesitated, like a child confronted by too big a choice of toys or candies, and then impulsively grabbed a bottle of *Pepto Bismol* and unscrewed the cap. Closing his eyes, he threw back his head and took a long slow swallow of the sickly pale lilac liquid. Then he belched long and loud, making a satisfying resonance in the huge bathroom. Feeling comforted, he recapped the bottle and replaced it among the *Mylanta*, the *Tylenol*, the *Alka Seltzer*, the *Preparation H* and the dozens of others.

Creeping back into the bedroom, he checked that Barbara was still dead to the world and then dressed himself in a blue cotton tracksuit which sported his initials monogramed on either side of a coathanger logo on the pocket. Carefully avoiding the bedside rug, he slipped out through the sliding doors onto the patio. Outside, sprinklers were spraying fine curtains of water over the green velvet lawns and the swimming pool's undisturbed surface mirrored exactly the bland blue of the morning sky. David strolled towards the gates at the end of the curved driveway, patting the cream splendour of his new Rolls Royce as he passed the carport in front of the double-garage doors. Crossing the front lawns between the clumps of succulent flowering shrubs, he picked up the heavy roll of newspapers in their cellophane wrapper which the newsboy had hurled over the hedge as usual.

As he wandered back across the grass towards the patio slipping the sports section out of the wrapper, the sprinkler system gave an alarming gurgle and then made a high-pitched squirting noise. Next moment David and the precious Rolls Royce were deluged by a torrent of coarse, misdirected spray, like the huge soaking droplets at the start of a thunderstorm. David glared in dismay at the

9

unsightly blotches bespattering his treasured limousine. 'Goddamit!' he yelled, slashing at the offending droplets with the newspaper. 'Pissed on again! I gotta call that sprinkler man . . .'

# CHAPTER 2

Down near the train tracks along Santa Monica Boulevard, the bum with the grocery cart and the dog was also taking a shower, but not after all courtesy of Santa Claus's reindeer. He was rinsing his lank straggling hair under a leaking fire hydrant and giving his stained and broken teeth a going over with his dirty forefinger. Now and again he cupped a handful of water and held it out to his thirsty mongrel. Kerouac lapped up the water and whipped his wormlike tail in grateful appreciation. The tramp completed his *toilette* by flattening back his hair with a couple of handsful of water and by flushing his mouth with several noisy gulps. Then he wheeled his possessions across the busy street towards a huge garbage dumpster parked alongside the railway tracks.

'C'mon Kerouac, *gourmet* breakfast today,' he promised, grinning expectantly at the words BEVERLY HILLS emblazoned along the side of the huge skip.

The mongrel growled in anticipation and scuttled through the traffic ahead of his master.

When they reached the dumpster, Kerouac jumped up onto the junk piled in the cart and watched greedily while the hobo searched methodically through the giant heap of trash bags. It didn't take the bum long to find a capped paper cup full of cold coffee and three-quarters of a sugared doughnut in a squashed cardboard carton. Whooping with wild elation, the tramp broke off a bit of the doughnut and proffered it at the dog's snapping jaws. The morsel was gone in an instant.

'Good boy Kerouac. That'll help to build you up,' he muttered, eating some of the stale delicacy and taking a few appreciative swigs of cold congealed coffee. 'Later we'll take a look see if we can't find you some genuine protein.' While he finished the discarded doughnut and the coffee watched by the whimpering, lip-smacking mongrel, the tramp read out some week-old items of news from a scrap

11

of newspaper he'd found in the dumpster. 'Hey just listen to this, Kerouac!' he warned, as if teaching the dog to be thankful for its lot in the world. 'There's bin floods up in Malibu and riots over there in Pakistan . . . and hell, they tried to behead a cop in London . . . and what about this pharmacist in Ohio tried to set fire to his mother . . . and all just before Thanksgiving.'

The dog growled its disapproval, but more likely its disapproval at only getting one mouthful of doughnut rather than at anything anyone had done in Pakistan or London or Ohio.

The tramp wiped his mouth, savouring the taste of the hard doughnut and the gritty coffee. Then he roused himself, stuffed the newspaper in the pocket of his dilapidated hooded windcheater, and set off again. Kerouac sat on the squeaking trolley facing his master with a stare of baleful resentment at the paucity of the day's breakfast. Reaching a blocked intersection, the hobo threaded his way through the backed-up traffic, and as he manoeuvred the grocery cart up onto the opposite sidewalk, two elegantly dressed women in long black coats and white turban hats looking like a couple of entrants in a Greta Garbo competition barred his way as they attempted to hail a stranded cab.

One of the middle-aged mannekins wrinkled her aquiline nose in disgust at the stench emanating from the filthy hobo. 'Really Dolores, you'd think the police would do something about these dirty bums!' she shrieked, curling her crimson lips in disdain.

Her companion, whose powdered complexion had gone even paler, nodded dumbly.

The tramp picked his nose ostentatiously with two fingers at once and wiped them on his flapping hood. '*Enchanté Mesdames . . .*' he snarled, bowing low over his junk. Shoving past them, he gazed up at the hills to the north shimmering in the sunshine. 'Come on Kerouac,' he cried, suddenly filled with optimism. 'On the road! Let's hit the Côte d'Azur . . .'

12

# CHAPTER 3

In his magnificent tiled kitchen, David Whiteman sat on a high stool at the counter wolfing down his customary orange juice, Danish pastry and coffee breakfast while studying the sports pages. He was surrounded by gleaming copper kitchenware and by gadgetry – hobs, microwaves, double ovens, blenders, graters, slicers, freezers, juicifiers, electric can openers, a small television . . . The spacious kitchen overlooking the patio was equipped to satify even the most fastidious chef, male or female. David ate very quickly, as if he had to be elsewhere any minute. He crammed big pieces of Danish into his mouth and then took a gulp of coffee to render the pastry more chewable. Barbara's collie, Matisse, sat by the stool glowering as David read out an endless commentary of sports reports to no one in particular.

'Quite a way to go yet,' Dave muttered through a mouthful of soggy dough. 'Giants ripped the Redskins thirty-six to fourteen! How about that buddy boy?' He tore off a lump of pastry and held it down by his knee, his eyes still scanning the results.

Matisse bared his teeth and snapped up the titbit, nipping the tips of David's fingers in the process.

David snatched his hand away with a yell, blowing bits of Danish all over the kitchen and kicking viciously at the dog with flailing feet. 'Get outta my sight you sonofabitch!' he shouted. 'There's gratitude for you.'

Matisse slunk away to plan more elaborate revenge later.

A moment later Carmen, the Salvadorean maid, came in carrying items for that day's Thanksgiving Feast. 'Oh Señor Whiteman, what a nice new hump-suit you are wearing!' she tittered.

David blew on his smarting fingers and eyed the girl's pertly pointed breasts under her tight blouse. Her slim brown legs were revealingly clad in flesh-coloured tights under a very short pleated skirt and she wore a coquettish little bow at her throat and garish earrings under her sleek black hair.

'*Jump*-suit, Carmen,' he corrected her, brushing the soggy crumbs off the counter.

The girl tittered again and set to work on the festive preparations.

Barbara walked into the kitchen dressed in a pink and white candy-striped trouser suit and strings of pearls, with her straw coloured wavy hair set in calculated disarray. She looked every inch the capable hostess. 'Now Carmen . . .' she purred in her smoky voice, rummaging through the pages of the Spanish phrase book she was carrying. '*Limpie las . . . las . . .* How the hell do you say candelabras? *Las candalabras*,' she guessed, pouting tenderly at Matisse.

David took a gulp of coffee as if it were something stronger and peered into the newspaper. 'For Christ's sake Barb, the girl speaks good English,' he pointed out.

His wife waved her heavily beringed hands. 'I'm aware of that David, but I'm trying to improve my language skills so that if we go to Mexico I can deal with things in an *emergensia*,' she retorted, flipping over the pages with her crimson lacquered fingernails as she approached.

Dave ducked aside and fled to the refrigerator, trying not to catch the maid's roguish dark eyes. 'Where's Jenny this morning?' he demanded rhetorically.

Barbara turned to Carmen. 'Asleep I imagine . . . Carmen, *por favor vaya al mercardo y compra . . .*'

At that momen Max wandered in wearing nothing but plastic sandals and tiny silver shorts which revealed surprisingly muscular legs and enviable equipment slung between them. He was brandishing his video camera and recorder like weapons of war. 'The Family,' he announced solemnly into the lens, holding the camera at arm's length. 'Scene One. Take One. Preparing the Feast. Here we see my father Dave Whiteman and . . .'

'Get outta here Max!' David ordered as his son focused the camera directly at him.

Barbara swung round angrily. 'Hey, how the hell do you think Steven Spielberg got started?' she protested.

'How do you feel this Thanksgiving Day, Dad?' Max persisted.

His father slammed the fridge door shut and took a large bite out of another huge Danish pastry. 'How do I feel?' he echoed, reluctantly facing the camera. 'I just wish my son would stop acting crazy on this blessed day when we should all give thanks for our blessings.'

'What about guilt?' Max challenged.

David munched relentlessly at the pastry. 'Sure. We should all feel a little guilty when people are starving,' he agreed, brushing jam and icing out of his moustache.

Barbara smacked her phrasebook shut on the counter. 'Guilt? Guilt is useless,' she declared.

David rounded on her. 'Did your *swami* teach you that?'

She nodded. 'My *yogi*. Ran Bir.'

Carmen emitted a shriek of laughter and dropped a pile of sweet potatoes into the sink. 'Yogi Bir . . .!' she giggled helplessly.

Suddenly the front door chimes rang out like a call for peace and order.

Dave groaned and plonked his half-eaten pastry on top of the fridge. 'I thought this was a holiday,' he cried.

'That'll be the caterer with the turkey,' Barbara told Carmen. '*La porta por favor.*'

'Arrival of the offering . . . The sacrificial bird . . .' Max announced into his camera, following Carmen out into the hall.

As the perspiring little caterer crossed the threshold followed by his delivery boy carrying a huge turkey, a tall extremely thin girl of nineteen dashed through the hall in a pair of jeans and a tanktop with a beachbag slung over her shoulder. She paused and stared intensely into her brother's lens. 'Hi Max!' she called, as if he were lurking somewhere inside the camera. 'I'm off to the beach. If Stacey calls, tell her I'm on my way.'

'The Sister, Jenny Whiteman . . .' Max announced. 'The Princess home from college and off in search of . . .'

'No breakfast again, Jenny?' Barbara exclaimed, coming through from the kitchen and glancing anxiously at her daughter's protruding bones.

Jenny shook her head and grimaced. 'I'll . . . I'll have something at the beach, Mom.' Then she noticed David behind her mother. With a radiant smile she ran over and kissed his cheek. 'Hi Dad. Bye Dad!' she grinned and ran out of the house.

David shrugged gloomily and didn't bother to try and avoid Max's roving lens. 'It's crazy. I always seem to be waving to that girl,' he said in a hurt and puzzled tone. 'For years now she's been just a blur with a nice smell.'

Elated with this snippet of personal revelation, Max stood back and ceremoniously panned the camera to follow the turkey along the hall and into the kitchen.

Everyone gathered round to admire the bird on the counter.

David nudged the bald caterer who looked uncannily like Edward G. Robinson. 'You sure this bird is big enough?' he asked out of the corner of his mouth. 'My father loves white meat.'

The little man smiled nervously. 'Your bird is bigger than the Mel Brooks bird and he's got fifteen people coming Mr. Whiteman.'

Barbara stared thoughtfully at her husband. 'Is he nice, Mel Brooks?' she asked absently.

'A very sweet man, Mrs. Whiteman.'

Next moment Matisse erupted among their legs in a furious storm of teeth and barking and threw himself at the hapless caterer like a tornado. As the terrified man scuttled out of the kitchen, Max zoomed in on the wild dog.

'That goddam dog is gonna kill somebody one day,' David said through his clenched teeth, seizing the remains of the pastry off the fridge and flinging it at Matisse.

Carmen broke into a fusillade of strident shrieks, each apparently unconnected with the other. Barbara glared at her husband and then at her maid and Max whip-panned across to catch her displeasure in a huge unflattering closeup.

# CHAPTER 4

By noon, the jogging park off Santa Monica Boulevard had become pretty crowded with kids practising their baseball pitching and all kinds of outdoor freaks limbering or doing *Tai Chi* as well as with joggers of all shapes and sizes. Hidden out of sight next to his loaded grocery cart, Jerry Baskins lay in the shade of some thick shrubs dozing noisily and totally oblivious of all the healthy activity going on around him. Kerouac was standing on his chest, nuzzling his master's matted beard and licking his face hungrily. From time to time, Jerry stirred and waved his grimy hands around in the air mumbling, 'Let Jerry sleep you selfish little mutt . . .'

Eventually the ravenous brown mongrel started nosing into the tramp's ragged pockets in search of some morsel he might have overlooked or might be hoarding for lunch or dinner. Kerouac's desperate snuffles were punctuated by pathetic whistling noises as each pocket failed to yield the tiniest scarp of food. Again and again he renewed his efforts to wake his master, but Jerry just shoved him roughly away. Kerouac at last gave up and sniffed the air, his beady eyes bright with vigilant hope. All at once a faint whiff of edible matter reached his nostrils and his ugly little ears shot up as he detected footsteps slowly approaching along the nearby gravel path. Every sinew tensed, he pushed his way cautiously through the shrubs and peered out along the path.

A pretty-faced fat girl was waddling towards him sneaking guilty nibbles at a bag of fresh *croissants* she was carrying. Kerouac stared in rapt wonder as flakes of crisp *croissant* fluttered to the ground in the shafts of sunlight each time the girl took a bite. His legs trembled, his hair twitched and his wet nostrils flared. He turned and looked back into the shrubs. Jerry was now snoring and occasionally smacking his lips, which only increased the mongrel's hunger. As the girl's huge legs encased in skin tight jeans passed the bushes, Kerouac gave in to his unbearable appetite. Rushing out, he followed her and snapped up the crumbs she was scattering.

Hearing his frantic snuffles, the girl stopped and ofered the mangy little dog a bit of her *croissant*. Kerouac gobbled it up in a second and sat gazing fixedly at the bulging bag and whipping his tail in desperation. 'Wasn't that good?' she smiled, walking tantalisingly on her way again.

Kerouac sat rooted to the spot in a cruel dilemma. Whining softly, he looked towards the shrubs where Jerry lay in dreamland. Then he looked back at the girl. Hearing his plaintive cries, she stopped and whistled invitingly, rustling her bag.

Kerouac hesitated, torn between the snores and the whistles and the girl waddled off again. The mongrel scampered into the bushes and tried one last time to rouse his master, but Jerry cuffed him away and rolled over into an even deeper sleep. Kerouac whipped round and tore off up the path. Catching up with the girl, he jumped eagerly up at her ample thighs.

'Hey what a cute little mutt!' the girl laughed, bending down. 'Are you lost doggie? I see you don't have your collar on.' She glanced round as if looking for his owner.

Kerouac licked the flakes of *croissant* off her chin and her bulging teeshirt.

Giggling with pleasure the girl hugged him to her balloon-like breasts. 'Hey, I'm such a softie,' she confessed as Kerouac nuzzled under her ear.

The dog craftily pretended to ignore the crisp warm goodies in the bag and concentrated on giving the girl an affectionate wash.

Unable to resist him any longer, she swept him up in her arms. 'Oh c'mon home with me,' she cooed, feeling his thin ribs against her.

As she carried him homewards, Kerouac gave one brief regretful glance at the bushes and then breathed in the maddeningly delicious aroma from the bag. Man may not live by bread alone, but dogs were different.

# CHAPTER 5

The Whitemans' Thanksgiving Feast was in full swing. In the centre of the vast chrome and glass dining table sat the glazed and gleaming turkey in a colossal silver dish, surrounded by all the garnishes and side dishes appropriate to the grand occasion. David presided over the proceedings with an electric carving knife at the middle of the table. Behind him, a football game was playing silently on the television ignored by the assembled family and friends. Jenny sat staring vacantly at her empty plate with huge anorexic eyes as if willing herself to resist any temptation to even think about food. Max sat across from her and with his camera at the ready, smiling mysteriously. Opposite her husband, Barbara was busily fussing with a bowlful of bland looking mush she had whipped up for herself in the blender, while next to her, Yogi Ran Bir – looking like Ghandi with a beard – sat wolfing down a heaped plateful of everything as though he were expecting to embark on a year long fast the next day. Carmen shared the family celebration, frequently getting up to serve or remove a plate. David's mother and father, Sadie and Mel, sat at opposite ends eating with slow and silent reverence and frowning at anyone who dared to betray the solemnity of the occasion, especially at Lou and Sheila Waltzburg, two jovial and hearty eaters.

Finally there was David's business manager Sidney and his wife Pearl. Sidney sported a David Niven moustache and a Cary Grant hairstyle and he wore a shiny flecked suit which matched his lighthearted jocularity. Sidney was holding up for the guests' admiration a large photographic enlargement of a luxurious trailer park.

'This is our San Diego site folks,' he crowed in his nasal East Coast accent. 'We're talking five hundred units here alone.'

There were murmurs of approval from the diners.

David tried to coax his daughter into taking some turkey. 'Come on honey, have some white meat,' he urged for the third or fourth time.

Jenny shook her head. 'I ate at the beach Dad.'

Lou, who was a successful dentist, helped himself to some more breast. 'So what kind of people live in these trailer parks?' he demanded sceptically.

Sidney Waxman smiled. 'You got your nice retired people. You got your regular folk who are sick and tired of this rat race . . .'

David grinned wryly. 'Maybe I should move into one of my own trailer parks!'

Max asked Sidney to hold the photograph up higher.

David glared at his son. 'Max will you stop with that goddam camera?' he protested wearily.

The Indian guru was in earnest conversation with Pearl Waxman, a brown leathery Californian with Nancy Reagan eyes. 'Indeed yes, you can walk on the fire, on the hot coals . . . yes, no question,' he assured her through a mouthful of sweet potato.

Pearl uttered a squawk of delight. 'Hey Sidney, Yogi Bir here says he can teach me to walk on burning coals!' she rasped.

David helped her to more breast. 'Useful if you're a fireman, Pearl,' he quipped.

Sidney put down the photograph and resumed eating. 'Can he teach you to walk on water, Pearl?' he asked, grinning round the table.

The elder Whitemans frowned with evangelical disapproval.

Pearl pouted doubtfully. 'I have very small feet Sidney.'

'It is in the mind,' Ran Bir reminded them.

'That's small too!' Sidney joked, swiggering his Californian Rosé.

David turned seriously to the guru. 'I don't suppose you could teach my daughter to eat?'

Jenny scowled at him in embarrassment. 'That's a deeply neurotic question Dad.'

Barbara looked up from her grey mushy Thanksgiving

slop. 'Since we girls have such tiny minds it shouldn't be hard to teach us,' she told her chastened husband.

Before David could counter-attack, his silent father suddenly shouted 'Pass the cranberry sauce please!'

Barbara waved her sturdy arms. 'Carmen, *las* cranberries *por favor.*'

'It could help when you have to walk on the hot sand at the beach . . .' Pearl said, chewing thoughtfully.

David offered his parents more turkey.

'There's no more white meat,' Mel shouted, adjusting his deaf aid and looking as if he had been mortally betrayed. 'I told you I love white meat.'

Sadie shuffled her feet menacingly at the other end of the table. 'The pooch ate all the white meat,' she complained.

Barbara glanced sharply at her mother-in-law's wrinkled throat. It looked uncannily like the neck of a turkey.

David caught the glance out of the corner of his eye. 'I'm using another caterer next year . . .' he hastily announced, poking at the ravaged carcass in search of more breast.

Sidney waved his fork. 'Make sure you give me all these receipts Dave.'

'I'd like to try to walk on hot coals,' Pearl persisted.

'Hey, only if it's tax deductible!' Sidney warned.

Sheila turned to Carmen. 'And how is your family my dear?'

The maid shook her head sadly. 'Not so good Señora Waltzburg. My brother, he is trying to get up here to find a job.'

The dentist's wife blinked sympathetically. 'And what does he do?'

'He picks sugar cane Señora.'

'Not much call for that in LA,' Sidney laughed.

Lou Waltzburg leaned across the table. 'How are your teeth, Carmen?' he inquired solicitously.

The maid bared her fine white ivories. 'I think it is time for another cleaning, Dr. Waltzburg,' she simpered coyly.

The dentist grinned. 'Just call the office my dear. There'll be no charge,' he offered.

David was about to make a snide remark about payment in kind, when there was a sudden riot of barking and a commotion under the table as Matisse attacked Sadie Whiteman's feet.

'Matisse, stop that!' Barbara screamed, staring through the glass table-top at her wild pet.

'That dog doesn't like us, David,' Sadie complained, kicking about as if she had suddenly been affected by Saint Vitus Dance.

'That goddam dog doesn't like *anybody*, Mom,' her son retorted, buzzing the electric carver in an attempt to shoo the pest out of the room.

Barbara stood up. 'Matisse has a nervious complaint. We're sending him to a psychiatrist,' she exclaimed protectively, her prominent breasts swaying over the table with motherly generosity.

Max focused his video camera through the table top. 'Neurotic Hound Scene. Take One!' he announced dramatically.

David swung round on his son, pointing with the buzzing carving knife. 'You should be learning the hanger business, not wasting your time with that goddam thing!' he shouted.

Max refocused onto his father. 'I don't like hangers.'

David leaned over the turkey carcass, holding the ominously buzzing knife only inches from Max's spikes of crimson hair. 'It's hangers that feed you, hangers that clothe you, it's hangers that bought you that camera . . .!' he yelled frenetically, waving the carver with almost murderous intent.

Under the table, Sadie gave Matisse a vicious kick. The dog yelped and scampered out of the room, yanking the plug attached to the carving knife out of its socket. A tense silence descended over the gathering.

Ran Bir quietly finished chewing and blotted his greasy lips with a napkin. 'Perhaps we should all meditate for a while . . .' he suggested.

David dropped the silent carver into the turkey carcass and sank forlornly into his chair. 'Max . . . what's bugging you, son?' he pleaded. 'Talk to me. Just talk to me . . . man to man.'

Max let the recorder run for a few seconds, slowly panning round the motionless and silent guests. Then he jumped up. 'Cut and print!' he called out and hurried away with his equipment slung around his neck.

# CHAPTER 6

Towards evening Jerry Baskins was rudely awakened by a ball which thumped into the foliage above him and dropped onto his nose.

'Kerouac!! You sonofabitch . . .!' he yelled, scrambling to his feet and emerging from the bushes to the astonishment of the trendy passers-by.

The small bunch of kids who had lost their ball crept away, gaping in fear and suspicion at the filthy dishevelled wreck scratching his mane of greasy hair in the undergrowth.

Jerry called out the dog's name and again and then wandered round the paths of the small park, button-holing startled joggers and strollers. 'Hey you guys, you seen a little brown mutt . . .?' he inquired over and over again. But most people ignored him and ran or walked off immediately. At the drinking fountain, he accosted a large black matron carrying a colourful parasol.

'Well, ah saw a dog sure, but it was black and it was big,' she replied, rolling her huge eyes with mischievous *double entendre*.

Passing a trash can a moment later, Jerry's experienced eye noticed a discarded hotdog still in its wrapper. Grabbing it, he unwrapped it and wandered round the park waving it about and calling Kerouac's name in mounting desperation. But it was no good. There was no sign of the dog anywhere.

Later he shuffled despondently along Rodeo Drive peering into the chic stores and apartment lobbies as if expecting to find his mangy mongrel hiding there. The lavishly dressed passers-by stepped ostentatiously out of his way, averting their heads from the stench and the wild-eyed menace of the gesticulating hobo as he weaved among the crowds occasionally yelling the dog's name. Suddenly he caught a glimpse of a small brownish animal running into a shopping mall filled with exclusive fashion boutiques. Jerry ran through the mall, jostling startled patrons and knocking over potted shrubs. He ran up and down escalators and along walkways, closely followed by two uniformed security guards. Brandishing the battered hotdog, he ran through an open air restaurant sending tables, plates, food and cutlery flying in all directions. He finally cornered the dog on the mezzanine and approached it with the bait from the trash can. But the dog was obviously not Kerouac. It was some kind of cross between a King Charles spaniel and a dachshund. It cowered in a corner, snarling viciously and ready to spring.

Jerry leaned against a pillar gasping for breath and cursing Kerouac, prepared to take evasive action if the enraged hound attacked. Next moment he was grabbed by the guards.

'What's your problem?' one of them demanded.

Jerry shook his head breathlessly. 'I lost my . . . I'm looking for my dog . . .' he panted.

'He lost his dog,' echoed the guard, nudging his colleague.

A small crowd gathered to watch the guards frisk their suspect in a desultory fashion.

'That's right,' Jerry gasped earnestly. 'Unless he was dog-napped.'

Finding nothing of any value or significance in his tattered pockets, the guards quickly lost interest. 'Go downtown and take a shower,' one told him, wrinkling his nostrils in disgust. 'Just get outta here pronto and stop harrassing people.'

The cornered dog suddenly rushed between Jerry's legs and disappeared yelping among the feet of the crowd.

The bum shook himself free and backed away from his sneering young captors. 'Screw you guys!' he shouted defiantly. 'I'm a citizen of this goddam country too!' Turning tail, he fled down the steps and out of the mall, leaving the outraged onlookers staring after him with suspicious contempt. While Jerry Baskins stumbled gloomily along the darkening streets despairing of ever finding his faithless companion, David Whiteman's cream

Rolls Royce slipped noiselessly southwards along La Cienaga towards the airport. Jenny sat beside her father, her thin face lit like a mask by the greenish dashboard lights.

'I sure wish you could stay a little longer honey,' David murmured, patting her long bony hands.

Jenny gazed down at the dark hairs on the backs of his thick fleshy fingers. 'I'll be back for Christmas, Dad,' she promised. 'And maybe Jim'll come home with me.'

'Good. I'd like to meet this guy. You seem pretty serious.'

Jenny shrugged. 'It's hard to find somebody as nice as you Dad,' she murmured shyly.

Her father grinned and smoothered his moustache thoughtfully. 'What does he do, this Jim?' he asked.

'He's road manager for a rock group.'

David swung the wheel to avoid a baglady who was tottering along in the gutter. 'I sure hope he's not a drug addict honey.'

Jenny shrugged again. 'I guess he smokes a little grass and uses coke once in a while. He's perfectly normal.'

They drew up at a red light and David turned to her, his face furrowed with anxiety. 'Jenny baby, tell me you're not using drugs,' he begged her earnestly.

His daughter snorted with irritation and stared stonily at the lights of the streaming traffic crossing in front of them. 'I'm nineteen years old,' she reminded him. 'You've got to stop interrogating me Dad. You and mother both.'

They started off again and a 747 screeched overhead, its lights flickering in the glorious dusk.

Jenny opened a pack of gum and started chewing irritably. 'I mean, how can Mother fall for all those charlatans and gurus and people?' she protested defensively. 'It's all so sixties . . .'

David laughed mirthlessly as they set off again. 'Well, it's better than last year honey. She was off ghostdancing in the caves with Chief Elkbrain.'

Jenny sighed with horror at the thought of Barbara indulging in ethnic cultural pursuits with her blue-rinse cronies.

'You haven't said a thing about the new car sweetheart,' David scolded gently.

'It's very nice.'

He turned to her. 'You don't think it's too Beverly Hills?'

Jennu smiled and touched his arm. 'Listen Dad, you don't have to justify anything to me,' she assured him. 'You work damned hard for your money.'

Her father shrugged uncertainly. 'I don't know, but sometimes I feel a little guilty,' he confessed vaguely.

Jenny twisted a few strands of her long fair hair in her mouth while she chewed fiercely on her wadge of gum. 'Guilty? Guilt sucks,' she snapped.

Eventually they turned into the airport. David patted Jenny's bony knee. 'Now be sure and get a good meal on the plane,' he urged her, a worried frown creasing his forehead. 'Promise me you'll eat?'

But Jenny simply chewed her gum and said nothing.

Miles back up La Cienaga, the solitary figure of Jerry Baskins rummaged in a line of trash cans, searching for his supper as he swigged from a crumpled Budweiser can. 'You're gonna get your ass kicked Kerouac . . .' he growled. 'A dog is supposed to be faithful. Who the hell d'ya think you are running out on me? I'm warning you . . . You're an ungrateful mutt of a mongrel . . . You're a lousy son of a bitch . . . How d'ya think you'll survive without me? I mean . . . who the hell's gonna feed you?'

There were tears in the bum's eyes as he rooted in the garbage and picked out a half-eaten sandwich with salami and mayonnaise. He brushed off some dirt and started munching the appetising find. But it was no good. He had no appetite left . . .

# CHAPTER 7

The full moon hung high above the Whiteman residence casting deep shadows across the smooth lawns, the patios and the softly illuminated turquoise jewel of the still pool. The palm trees were motionless and the night sang with insects flickering and buzzing in the silver moonlight. Through the huge sliding patio windows, the interior of the house glowed with warm yellow light.

Max's bedroom was covered in mirrors, with a ballet barre fitted along one wall. Books were piled on crowded shelves and also in stacks around the edges of the room. A huge futon covered in brilliantly colourful pillows took up about a third of the floor and one wall was almost completely taken up by a state-of-the-art video and audio system. The sound of Tchaikovsky's *Swan Lake* ballet music swoped and dived around the room. Also swooping and diving was Max himself. Dressed in a red teeshirt and tutu with red tights to match, he was practising pirouettes and jetés while watching his multiple reflections around the walls in rapt upstretched arms; he resembled some kind of demented fire demon out of the *Rite of Spring*.

Next door, Jenny's room was in darkness, empty and silent. But around the angle of the house, Carmen sat in her modest room staring up at the moon and lazily blowing smoke-rings out into the magical night. The walls were covered with huge posters of pop stars and movie idols, and on the small portable TV a quiz programme host was working a pair of geriatric contestants into a frenzy of excitement fit to cause a coronary catastrophe. Carmen sighed, drew heavily on her cigarette and tossed her black hair over her delicately modelled bare shoulders as though she were trying to seduce the moon itself.

In the master bedroom Barbara Whiteman sat at her vast dressing-table clad in a low-cut silk *négligé*, smearing her face with a pale greenish avocado skin cream which clashed violently with her vermilion lipstick and her crimson nail varnish. David was sitting at the end of the bed in his kimono bathrobe, eating a snack out of the bedroom refrigerator and watching Johnny Carson with the sound turned down on the TV.

'I'm getting worried about Jenny,' he said, breaking a long silence. 'I think she's getting anorexic . . .'

Barbara smoothed more avocado cream over her statuesque throat. 'Anybody who doesn't nosh all day is anorexic to you,' she retorted in her smoky voice.

David swallowed another mouthful of apple pie. 'Why couldn't she go to school nearby?' he objected. 'There are great schools here in California. And who the hell is this Jim?'

Barbara tasted a tiny spot of face cream on her finger and grimaced. 'I'm sure he's very nice, Dave.'

Her husband frowned at the blandly grinning Mr. Carson. 'You think they're having sex?' he asked anxiously.

Barbara wiped her hands on a tissue. 'Now don't get upset, Dave. This is a new age for women.'

David swung round to look at her. 'You know a damn sight more than you're telling,' he said.

Barbara watched his reflections in her mirrors. 'I hope she *is* having sex, Dave. It's time.'

He got up and went over to her. 'Nice shoulders . . .' he murmured, gently massaging her neck and kissing her hair.

Barbara jumped up nervously. 'Must be the full moon,' she muttered, slipping out of his grasp and moving towards the bed.

David looked hurt. 'I'm just feeling sexy. Who cares what the reason is?' he protested.

Barbara sat on the edge of the bed. 'Well I'm feeling depressed,' she informed him with brutal frankness.

'Maybe it's too much of that meditation stuff.'

She shook her head firmly. 'Ran Bir's convinced it's an allergy Dave.'

He tried to laugh. 'So, maybe you're allergic to me!'

Barbara swung her legs onto the bed and gave him a reproachful pout.

He watched her in the mirrors. 'Are you happy Barb?' he asked casually.

'I'm content Dave.'

'Well, sometimes I wonder.'

She lay back on the heaped pillows. 'I'm changing Dave and that causes some stress.'

David nodded and glanced at his own image for a moment. His jaw was getting heavier, but his blue eyes were still very bright. He wondered whether the grey moustache maybe made him look older. 'Why don't you just take a couple of *Tylenol*?' he suggested, wandering over to his own side of the bed.

Barbara snorted derisively. 'I'm not even going to dignify that suggestion with a response Dave.'

David lay down and stared unseeingly at the TV. 'I'm worried about Max too. He seems confused,' he said in a embarrassed tone. 'I just saw him wearing a tutu.'

His wife slipped on her eye mask and snuggled up to him. 'It's just the age Dave,' she assured him complacently. 'He'll be okay. Goodnight.'

After only a few minutes, Barbara had sunk easily into a deep sleep, leaving David staring at Johnny Carson. He flicked through the channels for a while and then switched off the set and eased himself carefully off the bed. Barbara moaned quietly and turned over on her side. David turned down the lights with the dimmer switch and shuffled quietly out of the room.

Passing the kitchen, David heard Matisse stir in his sleep. He groped around in the pockets of the kimono and found a couple of broken dog biscuits. Next moment, the dog attacked his slippered feet growling and snapping with vicious relish. David flung the biscuits at the animal and ran lightly along the passage leading round the angle of the house, leaving Matisse devouring the titbits in his basket under the counter. As he passed Jenny's silent room, David saw a welcoming crack of light open around the edges of Carmen's door at the end of the passage. He paused and listened to check that the house was quiet and then pushed open the maid's room door and entered Carmen's bright little nest.

Carmen stubbed out her cigarette and flung her arms round her employer's neck, pressing her gyrating hips and her pointed breasts against his stocky body. 'Oh Señor Whiteman, I thought you would come tonight . . . it is so beautiful.'

He held her close to him, shutting the door firmly behind him with his heel. 'You must call me Dave,' he commanded, meeting her hungry lips with his own.

She went limp in his embrace. 'Oh yes Dave . . . Dave . . .' she murmured, retreating backwards and falling onto the bed. 'I am the most lucky girl . . . Oh Dave, bite my titties . . . Oh yes . . .'

David struggled out of his bathrobe and lay on the squirming maid, pushing up the long teeshirt she wore as a nightie around her waist. 'Now *Señorita* . . . are you going to let Dave in?' he murmured, nibbling her neck and rubbing her ears with his moustache.

Carmen giggled, panting as she pulled off the teeshirt over her head and wrapped her slim legs around his waist. 'Oh Mr. Whiteman . . . Mr. Whiteman . . .' she gasped invitingly.

'Dave . . . Dave . . . Dave . . .' he insisted with mounting rhythmic passion.

Suddenly they both froze in mid-thrust as something shook the door. They heard the furious whimpering and scratching of Matisse trying to get in for more biscuits.

'It's only the dog,' David breathed, heaving himself back and forth on his elbows again and devouring Carmen's red lips with his own.

Keening with frustration and fury, Matisse bolted back into the kitchen and out onto the patio. He sprang up at the maid's window as if maddened by the passionate gyrations of the silhouetted bodies now kneeling up on the bed and by the quickening moans coming from the open window. Then Matisse turned his crafty malevolent gaze onto the small yellow box fixed to the wall of the pool filtering plant. With cunning expertise the dog sat back on his haunches and then launched himself up at the box like a cannonball. Next moment a shrill oscillating wail broke the stillness as the Whiteman's security alarm was triggered, and all over the house lights snapped on automatically.

With a growl of satisfaction, Matisse scampered away to watch the resulting chaos from the safety of the dark space underneath the Rolls Royce parked in front of the garage.

In the maid's room David and Carman had been on the brink of a mutual climax of hot, sweating and throbbing flesh.

'Goddamit, it's worse than losing a sneeze!' David gasped, extricating his trembling body from Carmen's clasping embraces and feeling around for his kimono. 'Fucking alarm! Now the goddam cops will be here in no time.'

Carmen went pale. '*Mama mía*! I have no green card!' she squealed, wriggling into her teeshirt.

David feverishly tied the cord of the kimono firmly round his waist.

'You must go!' Carmen whispered urgently.

He stared helplessly at her and pointed to the awkwardly bulging bathrobe. 'Okay okay, in a minute,' he snapped. 'Damn thing . . . Never does what you want it to . . .'

After a few more seconds had passed, he looked reasonably decent. 'Okay Carmen, now don't you worry. I'll handle everything,' he promised and fled from the room.

As he rushed through the house, David yelled to Barbara and to Max to keep calm. On the front driveway he met two policemen with flashlights and a huge German Shepherd on a chain emerging from their patrol car just as a second car swept through the gates with its beacons flashing.

'It's okay officer, there's no problem here,' he called, clasping the front of the kimono tightly shut. 'I'm sorry you got a false alarm here.'

The cop with the gigantic dog grinned. 'We'll take a look around anyway Mr. Whiteman,' he said cheerfully. 'You never know these days.'

There was a suddem clattering roar in the silvery air and a police helicopter appeared low over the trees, its powerful search-light probing the lush gardens below. 'Hold it right there!' rasped a metallic loudhailer voice and David was bathed in a harsh white glare.

'This is my house . . . My house . . .!' he shouted uselessly amidst the shattering noise, holding the kimono shut against the whirlwind from the slashing rotors overhead.

Underneath the Rolls Royce, Matisse peered out happily at the commotion he had caused.

Max emerged from the front door wearing only his shorts and immediately started recording the drama on video. At the same time a small mini van skidded through the gates and a young man in overalls and a baseball cap jumped out carrying a toolbox.

'Alarm Company,' he announced nodding to the cops.

David rushed over to him. 'How often is this going to happen Lance?' he demanded in a distraught and weary voice.

There was a sudden explosion of growling and barking as the German Shepherd detected the collie lurking under the Rolls and tried to go for him.

Max immediately zoomed in on the snarling dogs. 'Close Encounter of the Fourth Kind . . .' he announced solemnly into the microphone. 'Take One.'

Lance shrugged helplessly amid the din. 'Sorry Mr. Whiteman, could be the humidity, or maybe some animal,' he yelled above the helicopter engine.

'Christ, you need an alarm for the goddam alarm!' David groaned, clutching his head in both hands.

Lance shrugged again, staring at Max's sturdy legs with more than detached interest. 'Well sir, you do have the *Econo System* here. If you upgraded to the *Fortress System* . . . that's much more reliable.'

They were interrupted by an extraordinary apparition that had just materialised on the driveway behind them. A very tall black man dressed in a short fashionable bathrobe was striding irrately towards them, waving his long elegant arms in defiance of the tempestuous downdraught from the helicopter. The four cops all turned and levelled their flashlights and pistols.

'You just get your hands off them guns,' boomed the intruder, his teeth flashing dangerously in his dark face. 'You're talkin' to Orvis Goodnight, Record Producer, understand? Monsoon Records . . . *Thelma and the Good-nighters, Little Jam Boy Earl* . . . Okay?' The man stopped and berated the startled onlookers like an old-fashioned preacher. 'Ah live right across the street, but do ah get service like this?' he demanded, waving his arms at the chopper, the patrol cars and the snarling police dog. 'No sir, ah don't. Two weeks ago some thief tried to break into my place . . . Took you cops twenty minutes to show up. One little car. No dog. No chopper. And ah know why ah don't get the protection . . . Ah'm black and blacks ain't supposed to get to live here in Beverly Hills . . . Ah mean, let one black man stop to tie his shoe or scratch his balls on Rodeo Drive . . . SWAT teams parachute on the brother and frisk him all over . . .'

Orvis gestured at the grand two storey residence looming in the trees across the road behind him. 'Ah spent three million dollars on that pile of stucco and ah want the same protection you're giving Mr. Whiteman here.' He raised his arms prophetically and roared above the wail of the alarm and the roar of the chopper. 'And ah'm bringing in more brothers and sisters to Beverly Hills . . . We gonna loosen up this place . . .'

Orvis's oration ended in a shriek of shocked terror as a black and white ball of fury erupted from under the Rolls Royce, flew past the startled German Shepherd and threw itself on the record mogul, snapping at his groin and shredding the hem of his stylish bathrobe.

'Ah'm gonna sue you Whiteman!' Orvis yelled. Turning on his bare heels, he fled back down the driveway and out thcough the gates with Matisse only inches from his backside.

'Come back here Matisse!' David bellowed after the crazed collie. He turned distractedly to the police sergeant. 'Can we get that helicopter out of here?' he pleaded.

The cop spoke into his radio and the helicopter switched off its searchlight and climbed quickly out of sight towards its base.

'Thanks a lot you guys and sorry for all the trouble . . .' David said sheepishly as he watched the cops and the dog climb back into the patrol cars.

Max recorded Lance as he came across the lawn from the back of the house having fixed the alarm system and loaded his tools into the mini van.

'Max, go to bed right now!' David ordered, noticing that the alarm technician was lingering and eyeing his son's considerable physical endowment under the skimpy shorts.

Max panned the patrol cars as they backed out through the gates and then swung the camera up at the moon shining serenely in silver splendour amid the brilliant stars.

# CHAPTER 8

Early next morning, Jerry Baskins's decrepit figure shuffled slowly along the quiet alley between the backs of the luxurious residences. The sun glinted enticingly on the turquoise pools, the outdoor jacuzzis and on the manicured lawns and freshly mown tennis courts shimmering among the cool palms. With an air of despairing weariness the tramp peered over walls and hedges and through wrought iron gates, halfheartedly searching for his disloyal companion.

'Kerouac . . .' he croaked from time to time, not expecting any answer. 'Kerouac you sonofabitch . . .'

He stopped at the back gate of the Whiteman residence and studied the garbage dumpster without much enthusiasm. Beyond it, through the grapefruit trees, he glimpsed the blue pool and the heap of smooth white stones recently delivered for the construction of Barbara's new Japanese patio and waterfall. Pensively he thrust his hands deep into his empty pockets and stared at the pool and then at the pile of stones and then back at the pool again. His weathered face took on a look of inevitable resignation. He leaned on the wooden gate and it swung open with a creak, like a magic portal in a fairy tale.

Seeing nobody about, Jerry wandered through and crossed the velvet lawn under the trees. He stopped by the heap of stones and slowly started picking them up and putting them into the pockets of his tattered pants and greasy quilted jacket. As the increasing weight of the stones began to drag his pockets down, a faint and mysterious smile gradually spread over his face.

David Whiteman was standing at his bathroom window shaving and talking to his plant manager in Tiajuana on a portable phone. '*Bueno . . . Muy bueno*, Jesus. Okay, I'll be down there in a few days to wish the boys a Happy . . . a *felice año . . .*'

Suddenly David caught sight of Jerry's heavily ballasted

figure edging its way out along the bending springboard over the deep end of the pool. 'Hey Barb, is that the new pool man out there?' he called to his meditating wife sitting cross-legged in the bedroom next door.

A torrent of Spanish and English poured out of the phone earpiece, but David's attention was riverted on the outlandish figure poised at the end of the sagging diving board. Suddenly he realised what was about to happen. 'Hey you out there . . . Stay where you are . . .!' he yelled.

All at once the figure leaped into the pool with a gigantic splash and sank like a rock.

Still clutching the phone and dressed only in his fake velvet kimono, David rushed out towards the patio. He bumped into Max who was on his way to the pool. 'Is that some weirdo friend of yours?' David demanded. 'Call the cops and the paramedics . . . Call everybody!'

Reaching the pool, David did not hesitate but dived straight into the water in a graceful curve.

'Is it Geraldo or Nigel?' Barbara called out vaguely from her lotus posture on the bedside rug.

Carmen came running out of the kitchen. '*Qué pasa*?' she cried, seeing the telephone handset floating on the chopyy surface of the pool still jabbering in Spanish.

Max hurried out armed with his video gear and began recording the drama.

Under the water, David was struggling to heave Jerry's heavily weighted body off the bottom of the pool. He managed to drag it across to the steps and then he started trying to manhandle it up to the surface, his lungs bursting with the effort and his heart pounding like a piledriver.

As they broke surface Max zoomed in on his father's gasping, choking face and then on the pale, matted stranger he was fighting to save.

Little Mr. Nagamichi, Barbara's Japanese gardener, came scuttling across the lawn pursued by Matisse who had been tormenting him in the herb garden. 'Quickly . . . quickly . . . CPR . . . give CPR . . .' he shrieked, staring through his pebble glasses down at Jerry's lolling head supported on David's shoulder at the edge of the pool. 'Quickly, kiss of death . . . kiss of death . . .!'

As Mr. Nagamichi helped to pull the hobo up the steps and lay him on the astroturf surround, Barbara stuck her head out of the bedroom window. 'Don't Dave! Dave you might catch something . . . AIDS or herpes or bubonic plague . . .!' she warned shrilly as they turned the failed suicide over onto his back.

Still gasping for breath and spitting out water, David waved his wife away and bent over the prone body to administer the kiss of life. After only a few inflations, Jerry coughed up a stream of chlorinated water and then vomited a stream of variegated muck that flowed down his chin and into his beard in a multicoloured lava.

His rescuer knelt up and glanced wildly around him. 'Carmen, bring some blankets and some brandy!' he ordered.

The gaping maid nodded dumbly and vanished inside.

Jerry retched horribly again and raised his head. 'Brandy?' he said hoarsely, wiping his chin with his sleeve.

'He live!' Mr. Nagamichi cried triumphantly. 'Kiss of death work!'

There was a sudden strident screech of sirens and the driveway was invaded by a convoy of emergency vehicles. A police car, an ambulance and a fire truck drew up in front of the house with their beacons flashing and their radios chattering. At the same moment, Orvis Goodnight drove his cream Corniche out of the gate opposite. He braked and watched the hubbub in the Whitemans' place with smug satisfaction. 'Ah told you . . . Didn't ah tell you?' he asked the world in general with a huge grin. 'That white man dog finally killed somebody!'

The police and the paramedics with their equipment, and Carmen bearing blankets and brandy, all converged on Jerry who was now sitting slumped against the side of the diving board looking very green about the gills. Meanwhile Max jumped around in the background, immortalising events on videotape.

Jerry took a sip of brandy and coughed raucously as if he were about to throw up his lungs. 'You got any Courvoisier?' he inquired, grimacing at the taste.

'Drink it,' David insisted. 'The guy's still in shock,' he told the cop kneeling beside him.

'How long was he in the water?' demanded one of the paramedics, shoving his way through the throng.

'Not long,' David said nonchalantly in spite of his shattered nerves. 'I got him out pretty quick and gave him CPR.'

Carmen gazed at her employer in wide-eyed admiration. 'You saved him Señor Whiteman! *Muy macho!*' she sighed, smiling dreamily.

Barbara grabbed the paramedic's arm anxiously. 'Please will you examine my husband?' she begged. 'He's had his lips on this . . . this man's mouth.'

'Good work!' exclaimed the paramedic, punching David's arm approvingly.

They all looked at Jerry, who was now taking a puzzled interest in the crowd surrounding him.

'Feeling any better?' asked David, aware of an ominous pain in his own chest.

Jerry pulled a face and gulped some more brandy. 'So what gives, *amigo*?' he croaked, wiping his filthy mouth.

'You almost drowned.'

'I know that.'

'Nobody dies in my backyard,' David said pompously, wringing out the hem of his kimono.

Jerry shrugged. 'If I'd known that I'd've gone somewhere else.'

Barbara had been keeping a wary distance, peeping over the policeman's shoulder. 'How the hell did he get in here?' she exclaimed. 'I didn't hear the alarm go off. Got to call Lance back in . . .'

Carmen draped a blanket round David's shoulders and held it tenderly in place.

' . . . Tell the pool man to check the water for bacteria,' Barbara prattled on, staring at the bum as if he were radioactive.

David patted the maid's hand. 'Thanks Carmen,' he whispered. 'Got some coffee?' he added pointedly.

The maid hurried into the house, unaware of Barbara's frosty gaze on her back.'

'I knew that Red Cross class would pay off.' David chuckled, glancing uneasily at his wife as he got to his feet.

'That bum is just drunk and disgusting,' Barbara declared without a trace of sympathy.

David stood aside to allow the paramedics to examine the interloper. 'He's a human being Barb. Where's your Christian charity?' he snapped.

Barbara curled her lip as she pushed her way forward. 'Don't you talk to me about charity!' she cried. 'I volunteer three days every week at the Free Clinic.'

David shook his head sanctimoniously. 'Really you disappoint me, Barbara.' He nodded down at the brandy-swiggering heap at his feet. 'There but for the grace of God go you or I, my dear.'

She sniffed. 'Just you speak for yourself, Dave. I could never sink so low. I'd sooner kill myself.' Suddenly the irony of her words struck her like a blow and Barbara retreated in embarrassment.

But Jerry grinned up at her sympathetically. 'The dame's right,' he said, draining the brandy from the kitchen mug and struggling to get to his feet. But the weight of the stones in his pockets and his weakened condition kept him immoblised.

'Just take it easy now,' David advised, bending down to remove the stones.

Barbara hesitated awkwardly. 'Dave, I have aerobics in fifteen minutes and brunch with Sheila at Nieman Marcus . . .'

He nodded. 'Okay honey, you go right ahead.'

Still she hesitated. 'You sure you're all right?'

David nodded again.

Barbara ran forward and bent down to put her arms round his shoulders. 'You're a hero,' she murmured, almost kissing his wet hair. 'And I'm just such a scaredy cat.' She put her lips to his ear. 'Maybe the police can take the guy to the Rescue Mission or someplace. He looks awful.'

David shrugged her away and resumed the task of removing the dozens of white stones from Jerry's bulging pockets. 'It's okay. Don't worry about me. You go,' he smiled, gritting his teeth at the pain in his chest.

With a worried look on her large face, Barbara patted his head and went off into the house to get ready.

'I could arrest the guy for trespassing, Mr. Whiteman,' offered the policeman.

'Then what?' David challenged, unloading more stones.

The cop shrugged. 'Back on the street I guess. But maybe the second time the bum'll get it right. Sometimes I think they'd be better off dead. Nobody *gives* a damn anyway.'

David stood up angrily and was about to protest at such open callousness when Matisse came running across the lawn. The dog came over to Jerry and stood wagging his tail and sniffing the hobo's sodden rags with friendly curiosity.

Jerry ruffled the collie's ears. 'How are you little *amigo*?' he muttered gently.

Matisse stretched up his head and licked the tramp's dirt-streaked face. David looked on in astonishment, ready to grab the animal's collar if it suddenly reverted to its customary aggressive behaviour. Max zoomed in on the touching little scene as Jerry tickled Matisse's nose and muttered reassuring words.

'Can you stand up now?' David asked, taking the last of the stones out of the tramp's pocket.

Jerry nodded and slowly hauled himself upright.

'What's your name?' David asked affably.

The tramp stared round at the cops, the paramedics and the firemen. 'Grace Jones,' he growled.

Max laughed with delight and shot a huge closeup.

David put out a hand. 'I'm Dave Whiteman.'

The tramp took it. 'Jerry M. Baskins.' He gazed appreciatively at the lawns, the trees, the house and even the pool. 'This your place, Dave?'

'Yeah.' David went over to the cabana behind them and fetched out a red Terrycloth bathrobe.

'You a gangster, Dave?' Jerry asked, wide-eyed.

David laughed. 'I make coathangers.' He tossed the robe to the tramp. 'Here, take those wet things off and get this on,' he said as tactually as he could.

The hobo examined the smart robe critically. 'I don't look so good in red, Dave. Got anything in blue?'

Carmen had just reappeared with coffee and more brandy. 'That is a brand new robe!' she cried resentfully.

Jerry glanced at the label. 'Brooks Brothers!' he exclaimed, apparently satisfied. 'I used to shop there myself.'

Without warning he loosened a string and his ragged pants slipped around his ankles.

'*Jesus Cristo*!' Carmen shuddered, crossing herself at the sight of the bum's unspeakable undergarments.

David, who was beginning to look a lot more the worse for wear than Jerry, frowned with disgust. 'Put his . . . his things in the washer Carmen,' he ordered.

Averting her head, the maid seized a pool mop and picked up Jerry's pants with the end of the handle. Jerry retired into the cabana with the bathrobe and threw out his underwear and shirt, while Carmen dutifully hooked the foetid items with her pole. A few minutes later, Jerry emerged from the cabana dressed in the red Terrycloth robe. It was much too small for him but it looked like a fashionable kimono on him and was a great improvement on what he had just taken off.

Jerry posed for the benefit of the assembled emergency service personnel and for Max's roving lens. 'Don't throw my things away *amiga*,' he said roguishly, winking at Carmen.

Carmen held the mop handle with its disgusting contents out in front of her. 'But Dave . . . But Señor Whiteman . . .' she objected.

'Put them in the washer,' David insisted.

Scowling murderously, the maid flounced off to the laundry room with her head in the air and holding her breath.

David took Jerry's arm. 'Would you like something to eat?'

The bum's eyes lit up. Suddenly he looked ten times better. 'What you got?'

'We have turkey, dressing, some cranberry sauce and sweet potato . . . Things left over from Thanksgiving.'

The hobo considered carefully for a moment. 'You got any *white* meat?' he inquired casually.

David found himself staring into Max's inescapable camera. 'That caterer stinks!' he snapped. Massaging his aching chest, he led his malodorous guest off into the house.

Half an hour later, all the emergency services had departed and Jerry Baskins sat in red-robed splendour at the head of the kitchen table which was laden with a generous spread of appetising leftovers. At his feet, the black and white collie sat staring up at him with shiny-eyed adoration. Carmen flipflopped reluctantly around in her plastic sandals fetching and carrying items from the refrigerator, while in the background Max focused his camera on the unexpected visitor as if he were the Prodigal Son returned at last.

'Who made this dressing?' Jerry eventually inquired, after munching his way through several helpings of everything.

David smiled proudly. 'My mother.'

Jerry belched critically. 'Too much onion.'

Carmen threw up her hands indignantly and hit her lip to stifle her annoyance.

'Well you could at least say thank you,' David suggested gently.

Jerry looked genuinely mystified. 'For what?'

'For the food.'

'Thanks.'

'And for saving your life,' David added resentfully. He was feeling shaken after his ordeal in the pool and was certainly looking a lot worse than Jerry.

Jerry shrugged ungraciously. 'Think my clothes are dry?'

'You can keep the robe,' David offered.

'You might ask me to thank you again,' Jerry grinned.

David laughed wryly and shook his head, while Jerry poked among the remains of the turkey in search of any scraps of breast meat. 'You're tough,' he muttered with a kind of grudging respect.

Jerry licked his lips, sat back and belched appreciatively as though he were at a Bedouin feast in the desert.

David leaned forward. 'How did this happen to you Jerry?' he asked with genuine concern. 'I mean you're an intelligent guy . . . How did you get this . . . this low?'

There was a pause while Jerry wiped his beard with a napkin. 'Well Dave, I was in love and it ended. I took it pretty bad. I was teaching acting at the time.'

David sighed. 'Ah, show business! They're all nuts.'

Jerry nodded bleakly. 'I'd been pretty active politically in the sixties and then I started acting. I was in love with a girl in the class, but she walked out on me and I cracked and then one thing just led to another.'

Carmen stopped rattling cutlery irritably in the dishwasher and stood listening.

'That girl was beautiful,' Jerry went on, gazing reminiscently into the garden. 'She was one in a million . . . She became successful . . . Very successful.' He paused. 'You might even know her, Dave.'

'Who?' David said eagerly.

'Linda Evans.'

Carmen dropped a handful of spoons and everyone jumped. '*Dynasty*!' she cried in rapture.

David looked startled and Max zoomed and panned in ecstasy.

The tramp shrugged dismissively. 'Got some more cranberry sauce?' he asked.

Carmen and David both leaped to serve him at once.

'It was just before *Dynasty*,' Jerry rambled on. His face, now a little cleaner after his ducking, suddenly looked shiny and innocent, almost like a baby's bottom despite its frame of damp and tangled hair. 'It was between *Big Valley* and *Dynasty*. I just got low after we busted up and for about a year I was in pretty bad shape. I drank a lot and used a lot of drugs. Then my younger sister died from leukemia . . .' He paused and dipped a cracker into the cranberry sauce Carmen had brought him.

The others stared at him in silence, devastated at his pitiful history. Max had stopped recording out of respect.

'That did it really,' Jerry continued, munching hungrily. 'I mean we'd been real close because we were orphaned so young . . . I guess I just lost all my incentive. I didn't care what happened to me. I just learned to survive on the streets . . . And so here I am.'

'I'm so sorry . . .' David whispered after a long silence.

Carmen's eyes glistened with tears and she tore off a strip of kitchen towel to blow her nose noisily.

Jerry eventually stood up shakily and tied the cord of the Terrycloth robe tighter. His face looked ravaged and careworn, yet reconciled to misfortune. 'Well folks, time for me to hit the road again, I guess,' he sighed.

'Where are you going to go now?' David asked, following him out onto the patio.

Jerry stared into the trees like Clint Eastwood scrutinising the horizon. '*Quién sabe?*' he shrugged.

Matisse trailed along, fussing around the tramp's feet as if anxious not to let him go. Out by the pool, Max resumed his shooting on a wider angle.

'I hope you won't try that stunt again,' David muttered, bending down to fish the waterlogged and silent portable phone out of the pool.

'That's a very personal question,' Jarry said mysteriously. He nodded at the laden grapefruit trees. 'Mind if I take one for the road Dave? I don't want to end up with scurvy.'

'Help yourself Jerry.'

The bum wandered over and plucked the largest grapefruit within reach. As he returned across the patio he stumbled and almost fell into the pool again.

David hurried forward to support him as Jerry clutched his brow as if on the verge of fainting. 'You sure you're okay? You know you could stay here for a couple of days if you like . . . Until you get straightened out I mean.'

Jerry squinted woozily at his benefactor.

David pointed to the cabana. 'You could sleep there in the cabana,' he suggested.

Max stopped recording and waited for Jerry's reaction with bated breath. Matisse sat between David and the tramp, wagging his tail and drawing his mouth back in a kind of encouraging grin. Carmen hovered by the pool, glaring at her employer with smouldering ferocity.

'Stay here?' Jerry eventually echoed in disbelief, a slow smile taking over his tragic face.

Carmen stamped her foot with a flamenco flourish and

disappeared into the house muttering insults and threats in her native tongue.

# CHAPTER 9

Later that afternoon Barbara returned home laden with purchases. As her Mercedes coupé drew up next to David's Rolls, she heard a noisy commotion at the side of the house. Unloading her packages and boxes, she suddenly saw Matisse dragging the little Japanese gardener through the flowerbeds by the sleeve. She shouted to her pet to behave himself, but Matisse paid no heed and continued dragging the unfortunate Mr. Nagamichi into a dense clump of shrubs while emitting fearsome *Hound of the Baskervilles* noises.

'God, I wonder if the Betty Ford Clinic would take a dog . . .' she muttered, picking up a couple of dropped packages and fighting her way through the front door. In the kitchen she found David sitting on his customary stool at the counter snacking on the remains of the Thanksgiving leftovers. 'Did the pool man come?' she asked, dumping her purchases on the worktops.

'No, and the goddam sprinklers are going crazy,' David replied through a mouthful of pumpkin pie and ice cream.

'So is the dog . . .' Barbara muttered grimly, loosening her blouse and popping her strings of pearls down inside out of the way. She kissed him on the forehead. 'That was a very brave thing you did out there today honey. I told all the girls in the class this afternoon.' She glanced through the window at the still pool. 'So what happened to the poor guy?'

Her husband swallowed his pie. 'He's in the hot-tub, Barb.'

Barbara stepped back abruptly, her face a mask of incredulity. 'You telling me that bum's still here?' she gasped.

He nodded.

She strode across to the wall phone. 'What's the emergency number . . . nine one one?' she cried, dialling with frantic fingers.

David jumped up and took the receiver from her. 'I invited Jerry to stay a couple of days, Barb.'

'He's not staying in my home.'

'In the cabana out by the pool.' David hung up and faced her defiantly.

Barbara's ample breasts heaved and thrust with alarming indignation. 'Okay, I'm calling Seymour to come right over now,' she threatened. 'You obviously need immediate treatment.'

David smiled, keeping himself between her and the telephone. 'Shrinks like Seymour don't make house-calls,' he retorted smugly.

They stood nose to nose breathing heavily, on the verge of coming to blows.

Finally Barbara stomped over to the worktops and started to unpack her purchases. 'You don't know a thing about the guy. He's a bum . . . a derelict . . .' she fumed, sorting cartons of live yoghurt, low cholesterol margarine and bran into separate piles.

'What about our responsibilities to our fellow men . . . our fellow persons . . . our . . .' David stuttered, getting hopelessly confused with the new non-sexist vocabulary.

'Men!' Barbara snorted, banging down a dispenser of artificial sweeteners. 'That bum could steal everything.'

'His name is Jerry . . .'

'And then murder us all in our sleep!' Barbara whirled round on him, her eyes blazing under their turquoise lids. 'Is that what you want, Dave? Another Manson murder?'

Matisse started barking again, but this time more like a contented puppy enjoying a game.

David wandered over to the window. 'Look Barb, Matisse *loves* the guy . . .' he said, pointing excitedly outside.

'That should be enough evidence for anybody,' Barbara retorted triumphantly. 'That dog loves *nobody*.'

'Look for yourself,' David insisted.

Out on the smooth lawn, Jerry clad in the red robe but with clean hair and beard combed perfunctorily into some semblance of order was teaching Matisse to do elaborate tricks. He made a simple gesture with his hand and the dog obediently performed a passable back flip, landing in a submissive crouch at the feet of his new friend.

Barbara stared through the window, shocked and speechless. 'He is going to give my dog *fleas*!' she finally managed to squawk, her eyes filled with icy hatred.

'Good,' David muttered under his breath. 'Let's hope they're fatal to dogs.'

# CHAPTER 10

That night the full moon shone down like a benevolent goddess on the tranquil roofs of Beverly Hills. Carmen sat at her window with her long cigarette, blowing smoke rings into the night with sensuously pouting lips. Max stood in front of his mirrors wearing nothing but a trench coat and a trilby, watching *Casablanca* on the video and wondering if he could persuade Lou Waltzburg to fix his teeth so that he could talk with a mushy 's' like Bogey. In the small cabana out by the pool, Jerry M. Baskins lay on the uncomfortable campbed David had rigged up for him, tossing and turning and half-heartedly watching a Ted Koppel *Nightline* show about homeless vagrants on the portable TV from the kitchen. In the master bedroom his host was also staring at the Koppel show with the sound almost off, while Barbara lay fast asleep under her black eye mask on the far side of the bed.

Eventually Jerry gave up trying to sleep and wandered out onto the patio dressed in the red Terrycloth bathrobe. He gazed up at the sky, drank in the scent of the fruit trees and cept off towards the dark kitchen.

A few minutes later, David came creeping along the passage towards Carmen's room. As usual he paused at the kitchen doorway, ready for the onslaught from Matisse. To his dismay he realised that he had no biscuits in the pockets of his kimono. Holding his breath, he listened to the silent house and then moved cautiously into the kitchen, making for the tin where the dog biscuits were stored. Suddenly he felt a hairy body in his path. He froze, poised for the growling, snapping attack. But to his amazement Matisse merely looked up, licked his lips contentedly and put his head back on his paws. Unable to believe his luck, David advanced to the refrigerator to see if there was any pizza left over from supper.

He'd hardly taken a couple of steps when he almost fell.

headlong over a bulky obstacle lying in front of the fridge. There was a muffled cry of surprise and Jerry Baskins stood up in front of him, a wild silhouette against the white refrigerator door in the moonlight.

David jumped sideways and switched on the lights. 'You!' he gasped, clutching his palpitating heart. 'God you scared me!'

The looming Frankensteinish figure yawned. 'Got any low calorie root beer?' he asked hungrily. 'I can't sleep on that damn bed.'

'Too hard?' David apologised, retreating uneasily to the doorway as if keeping a lookout.

Jerry shook his unkempt locks. 'Too goddam soft, Dave. I'm used to the sidewalks.'

David nodded sympathetically. Out of the corner of his eye he saw Carmen's door open a crack and then she peered out and waved to him to hurry up. He tried to signal to her by pulling a series of grotesque faces.

'You okay, Dave?' Jerry asked, puzzled at the dumbshow.

David quickly pulled himself together. 'Oh sure, sure Jerry. Here let me fix you a cream cheese and banana sandwich to take to the cabana. It might help you sleep . . .' he suggested, going to the fridge.

'I don't like eating in my room,' Jerry objected petulantly.

David laughed. 'Why not?' he asked, taking out the items for the snack.

Jerry shrugged helplessly. 'I haven't had a room to eat in for three years.'

David quickly put together the suggested snack on the counter and offered it to his guest. Grudgingly Jerry shuffled over and took a sceptical bite. He liked it at once and started munching away like a kid.

David grinned with pleasure. 'It's the onion in the cheese that really does it,' he explained proudly.

'Haven't had one of these since my Brooklyn days,' Jerry murmured nostalgically.

'You from Brooklyn?'

'Flatbush Avenue.'

David seated himself on the stool beside Jerry. 'I grew up around Ebbets Field,' he mused, picking up a few crumbs from the plate.

Jerry nodded. 'I loved baseball then.'

'Yeah . . . The Duke, he was my idol,' David recalled dreamily, his eyes shining like a child's.

Jerry chewed happily. 'Roy Campanella . . . Carl Erskine . . . Carl, he was a tough cookie . . .'

David swept up a few more crumbs frm Jerry's sandwich. 'Ralph Branca . . . Pete Reiser . . .'

Jerry nodded again and sank the last mouthful. 'I'll never forget that fifty-seven season,' he murmured reverently. 'Drysdale won us seventeen games and then they damn well moved the team.'

David shook his head. 'Tragic. I cried . . . I really did . . . I cried,' he remembered, misty eyed.

Jerry gloomily contemplated the empty plate between them. 'Can you fix me another one of those jobs to take away?'

At that moment they heard Carmen's bedroom door slam shut with a noise fit to wake the dead.

David listened a moment and then shrugged and went over to get more ingredients from the fridge. 'Did you ever try to get a proper job and go straight?' he asked, slicing a banana expertly.

Jerry watched his host's skilful hands with ravenous eyes. 'Let's face it Dave, I'm one of life's losers. I played the game and I lost. You get tired of playing a losing game.'

David nodded, as if he really accepted this assessment of the man's continuing failure. He pushed the fresh sandwich across the counter. 'You just need a little luck Jerry,' he argued. 'I mean, I was selling lingerie out of the back of an Oldsmobile, and if I hadn't gotten a little money out of my Uncle Morrie and if I hadn't walked into a bar in New Jersey just at the right moment . . . Well, I would never have got the hanger business going at all.' He munched his own sandwich thoughtfully. 'I mean, I was in the right place at the right time. And then they started building all the new motels, and the market for hangers . . . Well, the rest is history.'

With a rustle of silk, Barbara suddenly appeared in the doorway with her sleeping mask pushed up onto her forehead like a pair of motorcycle goggles. 'What the hell is this, an all night diner?' she rasped.

Behind her, Carmen's door opened cautiously and the maid stared malevolently along the passage.

'Well Dave, it's your colon,' Barbra snapped, grimacing smugly at the crumbs on the counter.

Carmen's lithe figure appeared in the doorway next to her statuesque mistress. 'And don't you drop food on the floor and make a mess for me to *limpiar, por favor,*' she added sarcastically.

They all stared at her in surprise.

'I thought . . . I thought I heard a rat,' Carmen declared, glancing darkly at David.

Barbara glanced at Jerry. 'Maybe that's what *I* heard.'

Jerry glanced at Carmen. 'I only heard a door slam someplace,' he said heavily.

Carmen flashed her eyes defiantly.

David cleared his throat nervously. 'We've got a lot of rats in Beverly Hills,' he said tactfully.

Jerry nodded and munched his sandwich as he gazed unblinkingly at Barbara's flushed and shiny face. 'Rats are everywhere,' he agreed.

There was a chasm-like pause. In the middle of the floor, Matisse yawned with boredom at this apparent stalemate.

Barbara patted her wavy hair into place. 'Dave, I'd like to talk with Jerry alone . . .' she announced.

Her husband waved the knife he was holding. 'Sure thing Barb, you go right ahead,' he replied amiably.

Barbara led Jerry out of the kitchen and into the living room. Matisse trailed devotedly behind them.

As soon as they had gone Carmen wrapped herself hungrily around her employer. 'Oh Dave . . . Dave . . . I missed you so . . .' she murmured breathlessly.

David gently disengaged himself from her embrace. '*Mañana chiquita,*' he promised.

She threw back her head obstinately and looked down her finely ridged nose at him. '*Mañana . . .?* That's not funny Dave,' she protested. 'It is too late. *Tengo hambre . . .*

I am hungry for you Dave . . . Come on . . . I want you to come now . . .'

In the living-room Jerry immediately made himself at home and sat in a giant overstuffed white leather chair, with his bare legs chastely crossed and his hands thrust deep into the pockets of his borrowed bathrobe. Matisse settled down at his feet and curled up in relaxed but alert devotion. Barbara, looking quite formidable in her full-length white silk *négligé*, took the floor with her red varnished toenails gripping the white carpet like the talons of some huge predatory bird.

'Jerry, I want to apologise to you for the way I behaved today,' she began in her dusky voice, occasionally raising a red fingernail to organise a stray wave of straw coloured hair. 'I have to admit that I objected to your presence here. Frankly your appearance scared me. There's something threatening about you . . .'

Jerry lolled in the vast cushions and stared impassively at the white apparition before him. With her red nails and green eye shadow and the black eye mask perched on her forehead, Barbara looked pretty threatening herself.

Barbara smiled sourly. 'Of course I realise that this is a very superficial reaction and I'm quite sure that . . . that underneath you are a person with sensitive feelings. And I want you to know Jerry that I am trying hard to overcome my middle-class Beverly Hills prejudices . . .' Barbara paused and walked up and down, the silk *négligé* clinging round her robustly curvaceous hips like the drapery round a classical sculpture. Then she turned with a slightly simpering smile. 'As my teacher, Yogi Ran Bir says . . . We are all a part of the same Oneness, the same electric universal tide which flows in and out and through everything . . .' She came closer to Jerry and her perfume drifted across him in pungent waves. 'As a human being Jerry I understand you and I respect you and I want you to feel the same way about me.'

Jerry stared blankly at Barbara's navel. At his feet, Matisse looked up sharply, instinctively aware of the approaching disaster. Suddenly Jerry released a tree-splitting fart which sliced through the air in a prolonged high-pitched rasp of sound like a chainsaw, before cutting abruptly off.

There was a stunned silence. Matisse's nose twitched. Barbara's nose twitched. Then she clasped her hand over her face and fled back to the bedroom in a storm of rustling silk. Jerry sniffed the air and nodded appreciatively. Matisse got to his feet, moaned in disgust and disappeared in pursuit of his outraged mistress.

In the doorway Max hovered with his camera, smiling with satisfaction at yet another bizarre encounter safely recorded for posterity.

# CHAPTER 11

Next morning David's cream Rolls Royce glided through Beverly Hills, along the fashionable streets thronged with limousines, shoppers and upwardly mobile business people. Jerry Baskins sat in the passenger seat, clad in a pair of jogging shorts much too small for his broadish hips and with the Terrycloth robe belted tightly round his middle.

With one hand on the wheel, David was talking on the modular telephone. 'Okay Jesus, talk to you *mañana* . . . okay okay . . . *mañana*.' He clicked the phone off and turned onto a wide boulevard.

Above them, Santa Claus after Santa Claus leaped across the traffic. The jolly old rogues' cheeks reminded Jerry of Barbara's breasts the night before in the living-room.

'This your first ride in a Roller?' David asked casually.

Jerry shook his head. 'I had one when I lived in London,' he said nonchalantly.

David looked at him in astonishment. 'You lived in London?'

'Sure Dave. When I went to graduate school.' Jerry glanced at a smart menswear store they were just passing. 'What sort of hangers do you make?' he suddenly asked.

David flipped open the spacious glove compartment on the passenger side and took out a gold plated coathanger which he handed to Jerry.

'Congratulations to Mr. David Whiteman, President of DAVE-BAR,' Jerry recited. 'This gold hanger honors your sale of one million hangers to the Holiday Inns Hotels Corporation.'

David chuckled proudly and swung the wheel. 'That's the baby that revolutionised the business!' he cried, opening the sunroof a little further. 'It's got a magnetic lock. We make that baby in my Tiajuana plant.'

As they stopped for a left turn red light, an identical cream Rolls purred up beside them with Orvis Goodnight at the wheel. He was wearing a pink suit, a lemon shirt, a white tie and a straw hat. Rock music was blaring from the stereo.

'Mornin' Dave,' boomed Orvis patronisingly.

'Morning Orvis,' sang David without looking round.

Orvis gaped incredulously at the bizarre figure beside his neighbour. As soon as the light changed, he zipped away in a hush of white-walled tyres as if afraid of contamination from the wild-maned hobo.

David parked outside *Umberto's Hair Salon* and led Jerry inside. Trendy music pulsed from hidden speakers as they strolled in and nobody paid the slightest attention to Jerry's extraordinary getup. A dozen or so punkish and stylish young people were lounging around in the comfortable waiting area reading magazines and sipping cool drinks, while others sat side by side at the baroque framed mirrors having their hair created by a team of outrageous male hairdressers. David steered his *protégé* straight over to Maurice, an extremely camp black man dressed in a short-sleeved safari suit with a flower behind his ear.

'Ah, Monsieur David . . . How nice to see you again,' lisped Maurice. 'And this is the gentleman you spoke of is it?' Maurice smiled and showed the whites of his eyes in amazement.

David nodded and introduced them.

'Charming . . .' breathed Maurice, sitting Jerry in the chair and running his slim fingers through the wiry mess. 'Monsieur has the vagabond look . . . *Très chic* . . .'

'Just clean him up, okay?' David ordered brusquely.

The hairdresser sighed and muttered to himself in his sibilant singsong voice, forcing the comb through Jerry's clean but inextricably tangled hair. 'What do we have here?' he wondered despairingly. 'The Chinese bird's nest? I shall have to sterilise everything . . .' Maurice gazed at his client's sceptical, uncooperative features in the tinted gold-framed mirror. 'We can do the Bob or the layered Bob . . . or the Wedge . . . the Shag . . . the Pussy . . . the *Coup Sauvage* . . .' he lisped.

Jerry slid gloomily down into the chair. 'Just give it the

Mongrel, Maurice,' he snapped in exasperation. 'Give it the Kerouac.'

Several hours later, after visits to a couple of the most fashionable menswear stores on Rodeo Drive, Jerry climbed out of the Rolls at the entrance to the DAVE-BAR hanger factory. His wild beard was gone, though he sported a moustache now neatly trimmed and his hair had been drastically cut and styled with Maurice's loving care. His face looked a little lost without its frame of mangy tangles, and the newly exposed skin around the jaw was pale and puffy. But the bum had been transformed into a fairly flashy and trendy citizen. David had kitted him out in a fashionable blouson style shirt, tapered pants with zips and pockets all down the legs and white socks and boots.

Walking awkwardly and uncomfortably in his unfamiliar clothes, but looking sleek and almost debonair despite his unease, Jerry followed the successful industrialist around the modern factory. The plant was grey and noisy inside, full of constantly humming machinery and rattling conveyor belts thickly clustered with thousands of wire coathangers of all shapes and sizes.

'Five hundred thousand hangers a day . . .' David shouted above the din as he guided Jerry past machines relentlessly uncoiling, bending, twisting, shaping, painting and drying the endless wire.

There were only about twenty human operatives visible in the entire operation.

'Five hundred thousand and we're talking four cents a hanger,' David enthused, leading the bewildered Jerry by the arm. 'I don't need salesmen Jerry . . . No salesmen . . .'

They passed a young guy chewing gum as he monitored the operation of a large paint-spraying rig.

'How you doing, Bobby?' the proprietor shouted, slapping his employee heartily on the shoulder.

Bobby nodded hello without taking his eyes off the machine.

'This is where DAVE-BAR started,' Jerry's guide

continued, waving his arms around. 'Hey, how you do Raymondo?'

Raymondo, a squat Puerto Rican in a singlet, grinned happily as he tossed a reject over his shoulder into a skip filled with failed hangers.

'Hey not too many now, Raymondo!' the boss quipped with mock disapproval.

'It's a lot of hangers . . .' Jerry agreed, gazing around him with a dazed expression.

'And now I'm negotiating with the Chinese!' David shouted, pausing to adjust a conveyor speed control and then setting off again with boundless enthusiasm. 'We're throwing a New Year Party for their Trade Minister . . . Minister Chan and his outfit. Imagine it Jerry, a billion Chinese . . . Twenty five million hangers minimum! Those Chinese are very neat.'

Jerry nodded pensively. 'You hardly ever see a Chinese bum.'

David led the way through into the relative clam and quiet of the packaging and dispatch area. 'You want a job Jerry, I can start you tomorrow,' he offered with an expansive sweep of the hand. 'You can do the assembly line or you can get your feet wet in shipping!' He threw back his head and roared with laughter.

Jerry stared blankly at the stacks of cardboard cartons. 'Not really my line, Dave,' he mumbled, smiling wanly.

But David was off again, bearing down on another little Puerto Rican who was collecting finished hangers from the conveyor on his straightened arm, counting them at a glance and sliding the armful deftly into the waiting carton. The man worked with the simple economic precision of a machine.

'We got a really fine health plan here,' David boasted. 'Just started up a comprehensive dental scheme . . . Hey Carlos, show him your new teeth!'

Without interrupting the sequence of his movements, the little packer opened his mouth and flashed a dazzling set of dentures.

'You need to think about things like that Jerry,' David declared solemnly, inspecting some palleted cartons.

Jerry walked over and seized his arm with almost desperate urgency. 'Can we grab some lunch, Dave?' he begged, his stomach rumbling and whistling under his new finery.

David grinned generously. 'Sure thing *amigo. Vamos . . .*'


David drove Jerry back to Beverly Hills for lunch at *Le Petit Kyoto*, a trendy outdoor cafe on Sunset Boulevard where nouvelle cuisine delicacies were served by cute Japanese waiters and waitresses. Over the stereo system, Tangerine Dream were playing Vivaldi as little Mr. Yamato, the proprietor, personally showed David and his guest to a table by the entrance, where they could study the show-business clientele arriving and handing their keys to the Parking Valets before parading in among the tables. In the background, hidden among palms and baskets of flowers, several pop stars and movie celebrities gossiped over their pricey morsels.

'Here we are Mr. Whiteman. *Asparagus Nagasaki* and *Chicken Kyoto*,' Yamato purred, setting two minute portions in front of his favoured clients.

Jerry bent forward and peered closely at his microscopic helping. 'Looks more like *Chicken Hiroshima* to me.' he growled in scandalised disappointment, flinging aside the dainty floral garnish and seizing his tiny fork with murderous intent.

David smiled up at Yamato and poked at his own Lilliputian entrée with fastidious appreciation. 'This is the new *in* place, Jerry. Show-business and all that. My wife comes here.'

Mr. Yamato's eyes widened as he suddenly caught sight of Jerry's bare feet under the table. While they had been waiting for their lunch to be served, Jerry had slipped off his shoes and his socks and was airing his feet and wiggling his toes. Some hornrim-spectacled film studio executives at the neighbouring table were also staring at the white, fish-like feet with distaste.

'Another bottle of the *Beaujolais* Mr. Whiteman?'

Yamato inquired with hushed civility, trying to create a diversion.

'What do you say Mr. Baskins?' David laughed, nudging his guest and unaware of the scandal underneath the table.

Jerry sucked his lips and stared at his empty little plate. 'No, but I sure could use another piece of chicken,' he said wistfully.

As Yamato glided away to attend to the order, a stunningly beautiful girl with faintly Arabic looks strolled into the restaurant. Her breasts swung riotously to and fro inside her loose jersey which was tightly belted into her calf-length slacks. She stopped and stared at Jerry as if she recognised him from somewhere.

Jerry winked and David gasped in admiration and amazement.

'Didn't I see you at the Cannes Festival?' the girl asked, thrusting her tits over Jerry like a protective awning.

Jerry grinned and nodded. 'Sure you did.'

The girl shoved her sunglasses onto her forehead. 'Yeah, you were with Susan Sarandon . . . Something to do with Nicaragua. Are you a Sandinista?'

Jerry widened his grin and shook his head.

The girl frowned and then smiled. 'I know . . . You're Sandy Kinney's boyfriend. You're a writer . . . But I don't remember your name.' '

'Jerry Baskins.'

'That's right. Jerry Baskins.' The girl held out her hand. 'Roxanne . . . Roxanne Philobosian.'

Jerry took the hand and licked the backs of the long fingers like a dog. David sat back and watched, impressed.

'My pleasure, Roxanne,' Jerry drawled lazily. 'Oh and this is my friend Dave Whiteman.'

The girl flashed her almond eyes at the speechless coathanger magnate. 'Hi!' she said. Then she turned back to Jerry. 'Listen, I'm at MGM now. Call me if you get any story ideas. We're really on the lookout right now.' She handed him a small business cad. 'Here's my card. And say hi to Sandy. Bye Dave . . .'

David followed the gorgeous lady to her table with his eyes and then looked at Jerry with a new expression of wary respect. 'So you're a writer?' he exclaimed, stroking his moustache and wondering just how much people could infer from his own appearance.

Jerry had been squinting at the card Roxanne had given him. Suddenly he caught sight of a familiar figure shuffling past on the sidewalk in newspaper and garbage-bag footwear with a strangely robotic skiing motion. 'Hey Al! . . . Al, it's me!' he shouted, leaping up and almost overturning the table in his excitement.

David looked up and saw Jerry gesticulating at a filthy derelict, a tall black guy wearing a baseball cap and an incredible motley of stinking rags. The bum stopped shuffling and glanced up at the sky as if hearing voices.

'Al! . . . Over here . . .!' Jerry shouted.

The bum peered over the low hedge dividing the tables from the sidewalk and then stared at Jerry with wild bloodshot eyes. David gasped as the hobo's pungent odour invaded his nostrils with overpowering intensity and he groaned in dismay as Jerry went over and brought the tall pile of rags into the restaurant. The other patrons recoiled in shock as the hobo shuffled past their tables beaming at everyone, the stench rising from his body in almost visible waves like a heat haze.

'You sure it's okay, Jerry?' Al croaked as he was led to David's table.

'Sure thing Al,' said Jerry kindly. 'Hey Dave, is it okay if Al here joins us?'

David forced himself to his feet and shook Al's huge dirty hand. 'Why not Jerry?' he heard himself reply. 'He's a human being just like you and me. Dave Whiteman . . .' he grinned into the lugubrious face looming over him.

'Al.'

Mr. Yamato hovered nearby with Jerry's second order of chicken, looking as if he wished the ground would open and swallow the table and the three guests. The other customers shrugged and went back to their meals, having convinced themselves that the newcomer must be some kind of eccentric billionaire.

'You sure look different . . .' Al mumbled, gazing in wonder at Jerry's new image. 'I hardly recognize you man.'

Jerry laughed selfconsciously. 'Yeah Al, well, the hair and the beard I guess . . .'

'And the gear!' Al fingered his friend's new shirt from I. Magnin. 'Christ man, I thought I was hearin' voices back there.'

Just then a passing busboy dropped a half-eaten roll on the floor. With an incredibly fast dive, Al snatched it up and crammed it into his mouth. It was a virtuoso feat, accomplished with nonchalant expertise.

Mr. Yamato sidled up and served Jerry's second portion of *Chicken Kyoto*. David asked him to bring another chair for Al. 'You want to eat, Al?' he asked.

'No thanks,' Al said, munching his roll.

Averting his face as tactfully as he could, Mr. Yamato brought a third chair for Al. The derelict dropped into it and plonked his elbows on the white starched cloth.

Yamato looked ready to faint. 'Are you by any chance expecting any more . . . any more guests Mr. Whiteman?' he asked in a strangled voice.

David slipped him a twenty dollar bill. 'I think this is about it, Yamato. Some wine Al?'

The hobo shook his head. 'This is one of my nondrinking days Dave,' he said firmly.

With a sigh, Mr. Yamato threw up his hands and departed.

'Al and I were down at the Mission together,' Jerry explained to David.

Al nodded grimly. 'Remember Red Turner . . . the redheaded guy with the glasses? He got mugged real bad. He's in County Hospital.' Glimpsing a fallen asparagus shoot by David's foot, Al swooped down and swept it into his cavernous mouth.

David touched Al's disintegrating sleeve tentatively. 'They make a great club sandwich here Al,' he suggested hopefully.

'Red Turner must be pretty old,' Jerry remarked, staring at the juice dribbling down Al's chin.

There was a silence.

Al abruptly got up, picking a piece of chicken off David's plate. 'Well, it was good to see you again Jerry, sitting so pretty . . . Yeah . . . Yeah . . . Gotta go . . . See you guys . . .' And he shuffled out of the restaurant on his huge plastic and paper 'shoes'.

'Where's the guy going?' David demanded, both relieved and disappointed at the bum's abrupt departure.

Jerry shrugged mysteriously. 'He has his schedule too, Dave.'

David swilled the last of the *Beaujolais* round in his glass and drained it. 'No offence Jerry, but some of these street guys do seem just a little crazy.'

Jerry picked up the remains of his chicken and swallowed it in one bite. 'Well Dave . . . A lot of the guys you see on the street are talkin' to someone that you'll never meet . . .' he mused in an unintentional rhyming couplet.

David sat in silence for several minutes, touched by Al's brief appearance and intrigued by the mystery of the vagrant existence. Then he roused himself and smiled. 'Now then Jerry, what about some chocolate mousse?' he suggested, more cheerful again. 'It's only around thirty five bucks a shot here!'

# CHAPTER 12

Barbara and Carmen sat on the gigantic white leather sofa in the living room watching Matisse with intense concentration. The dog was sitting on the long fleecy rug refusing to acknowledge the existence of a loaded plate of dogfood in front of him. In the overstuffed armchair sat Dr. von Zimmer, a bald animal psychologist in his late thirties, who sported an earring, heavy hornrimmed glasses and a red bowtie with a tartan shirt and light suit. Von Zimmer was gazing fixedly at Matisse as if trying to out-stare the dog.

Eventually Von Zimmer broke the long, unproductive silence. 'Matisse . . . What a pretty dog,' he said in a sort of hybrid voice which was a combination of gutteral and nasal.

The dog did not react.

Barbara murmured anxious warnings as the psychologist slowly leaned forward as if about to attempt to hypnotise his patient.

Matisse uttered a throaty growl and bared his teeth.

Von Zimmer began to make faint whimpering sounds in imitation of a dog in distress.

Matisse yawned with derision and kept his eyes on Von Zimmer's.

All at once, David and Jerry strolled in laughing and chatting like buddies returning from a round of golf.

'Ssssh Dave . . .!' Barbara hissed, smiling apologetically at the psychologist.

'What the hell's going on?' David demanded.

'Dr. von Zimmer is here.'

David's eyebrows shot up in anticipation. 'Did the dog bite Orvis?' he asked hopefully.

Barbara whirled round in her seat. 'I don't suppose you've even noticed, Dave, but Matisse hasn't eaten in three days,' she informed him tearfully.

Her husband shrugged. 'Let's face it Barb, we've got an anorexic dog.'

Von Zimmer turned his serious brown eyes on the newcomers. 'The dog is disturbed, he rasped ominously. 'Something is bothering Matisse. He is angry.'

'That dog is always angry,' Dave scoffed, bending to give his wife a peck on the back of the neck.

Von Zimmer rose authoritatively to his feet. 'You would be surprised how the tone of your voice can affect animals,' he said accusingly. He turned to Barbara. 'Mrs. Whiteman, has anything recently changed in the dog's routine or in his living arrangements?' he asked critically.

Barbara nodded towards Jerry, who was lingering in the doorway watching the immobile, silent Matisse with sympathetic sadness. 'Well, we have . . . we have a house guest here, Dr. von Zimmer.'

The psychologist scrutinised Jerry suspiciously for a few seconds and then bowed his head and placed the palms of his hands together as if in prayer. 'That explains it,' he said with a cold smile. 'This is very traumatic for the doggie. A new face, a new voice, new smells . . .'

Barbara's nose wrinkled as if in memory of certain new smells. 'How about for me?' she murmured quietly.

Von Zimmer went over to her. 'Give it another day Mrs. Whiteman,' he advised confidentially. 'Deny all food until the evening. Then give me a call. But I can't promise anything at this stage.' He glared at Jerry. 'How long will you be staying here?' he demanded.

Jerry glanced at David and at Barbara and lastly at Carmen and then shrugged.

'Dr. von Zimmer, Jerry is staying here just as long as he likes,' David declared defiantly. 'And if the doggie doesn't like it, *he* can find new living arrangements.'

Barbara's breasts rose and fell tempestuously under her open knitwork sweater.

'The dog senses your hostility,' von Zimmer told David with a spiteful gleam in his eyes. 'That is cruel. You soil its *Weltanschauung*! Now you have to go and caress the dog and reassure him.'

David stared at the animal shrink in outraged disbelief. 'I what?' he exploded.

Barbara grasped his hand angrily. 'Dave!' she warned.

'That damn dog is running this house . . .' David muttered through clenched teeth, reluctantly approaching the cowering Matisse.

'Good. Now caress. Speak. Reassure . . .' von Zimmer commanded in a whisper.

David forced himself to bend down and ruffle Matisse's lank ears. 'What a nice dog . . .' he snarled. 'What a good dog . . .'

Von Zimmer nodded to Barbara and clasped her hands encouragingly: 'As soon as your . . . your guest departs dear lady the dog will be ravenous,' he prophesied.

David glared at Matisse's smugly grinning mouth. Utterly humiliated, he rose and stepped backwards. Carmen emitted a shriek of hysterical glee and Barbara turned in the act of shaking von Zimmer's hand to see her husband hopping round and round Matisse with the plate of dogfood stuck to the sole of his silver-buckled shoe.

# CHAPTER 13

The departure of Dr. von Zimmer was the signal for Matisse to rush out of the house leaving the trodden plate of food sitting in the middle of the fluffy carpet like a stranded prop in an abandoned TV Commercial. He tore across the patio, skirted the pool and shot across the lawns under the trees and up to the fence which divided the Whiteman property from that of their Iranian neighbours. Then he stood and barked ferociously up at the tall minaret which the Iranians were having constructed at the corner of their onion-domed and gold-mosaic-decorated residence. The workmen on the scaffolding around the top of the minaret glanced down and flourished their hammers in the ritual daily confrontation with the Whiteman hound.

After a while, an almond-eyed boy of about fifteen with delicately modelled features and jet black hair looked over the fence and stared at the frenzied dog with a puzzled and plaintive expression. Matisse stopped barking for a moment as if outraged at such barefaced impudence. Then he resumed his raucous onslaught with redoubled ferocity.

The boy was about to retreat back to the house, which resembled a spanking new mosque set in some exotic Persian grove, when Jerry wandered over to the fence dressed in bathing shorts with a jazzy towel round his shoulders. 'Hey quiet Matisse. Sit!' he ordered.

Matisse sat and fell silent.

'He's only trying to say hallo,' Jerry explained, speaking with slow and deliberate emphasis. 'Do not be afraid.'

'Hallo,' the boy replied happily. 'Thank you very much, sir.'

Jerry studied him for a second. 'Are you Iranian?' he asked.

The boy's eyes clouded defensively. 'Yes, sir. But we live here now in Beverly Hills,' he said with cultured politeness.

Jerry smiled and introduced himself.

The boy smiled back. 'My name is Akbar . . . Akbar Masoud.'

Jerry gestured at the Whiteman's fruit trees behind him. 'Want an apple, Akbar?'

The boy's sad eyes brightened as if he'd been offered treasure. 'Thank you, Jerry. I would like an apple.'

Jerry strolled over and picked three of four golden apples. 'There you are Akbar,' he said with exaggerated *largesse*. 'Just help yourself any time.'

The boy glanced apprehensively at Matisse and then nodded and smiled at Jerry.

Jerry waved kindly and strolled back across the lawn to the patio jacuzzi. Whistling cheerfully, he plunged in and turned everything on full. Matisse trailed submissively after his adopted master and sat quietly at the edge of the foaming whirlpool watching Jerry enjoy his bathe with adoring eyes. Jerry soon dozed off in the soothing swirl of scented water. Matisse lost interest and wandered off into the house.

The dog found a new target in the kitchen in the form of the Sparkletts Man, who was hurriedly fixing the sodawater machine. He tore across the slippery tiled floor and sank his teeth into the man's frayed sneakers.

Barbara switched off the blender in which she was mixing herself a sludgey macrobiotic snack. 'Stop it, Matisse! Stop that this minute or I'll call Dr. von Zimmer!' she threatened.

But Matisse continued tearing at the dilapidated shoes with demented purpose until suddenly Jerry's dripping, lobster red figure appeared from the patio swathed in the jazzy towel. Matisse instantly went as quiet and docile as a lamb and the Sparkletts Man took the opportunity to beat a hasty retreat.

Jerry went to the refrigerator and took out a Michelob Light. Barbara stirred her grey gunge and tried to ignore the unwelcome house guest as he unzipped the beer and drank noisily.

Eventually Jerry nodded at Matisse's motionless, silent body at his feet. 'I was listening to you folks discussing the dog,' he said nonchalantly. 'I think I might be able to help.'

Barbara grunted and stirred her slop energetically. 'Dr. von Zimmer seems to think that you are the cause of the problem.'

Jerry gulped some beer and smacked his lips. 'Could be, Barb.'

Barbara stirred the bland sludge even more energetically. 'I mean Matisse has always been a picky eater,' she admitted, less sure of herself now. 'I do my best. I try everything. I've bought that animal every conceivable kind of dogfood.'

Jerry detected a hint of vulnerable desperation in her grating voice. 'Where is the dog's food?' he asked casually.

Barbara glared at him in resentful impotence and then gestured with her fork at the cupboard above the chest freezer.

Jerry finished his beer, crushed the can and flung it into the garbage bin. Then he wandered over and looked in the cupboard. The shelves were crammed with about thirty different brands of dogfood in cans, packets and sachets. Matisse watched with cynical detachment as Jerry took the different packs out of the cupboard and laid them on the kitchen table one by one.

Jerry frowned. 'You see Barb, this dog thinks it's a person,' he explained, like a teacher in front of an infants class. 'It doesn't have any dog friends or dog family. It wants to eat what people eat . . .' He glanced at the mush in the blender ' . . . except perhaps for that stuff you eat. You see Barbara, taste is very important.' Jerry picked up a couple of cans. 'Now *Mighty Dog* is pretty good, but *Gourmet Pup* here is far too salty.' Jerry took a can of *Puppy Chow* and opened it.

'How the hell do *you* know?' Barbara demanded as if she were afraid to hear the answer.

Jerry held out the opened can and Barbara winced at the sight of the jellied lumps of meat. Then she glanced at the sludge in the blender. Her snack definitely looked worse.

Jerry sniffed the *Puppy Chow* appreciatively. 'This is reall nutritious stuff. People take far better care of their dogs' diets than they do their own.' He tasted a spoonful of the *Puppy Chow* and smacked his lips. 'There's been many a day when I've wished I had a plateful of this to munch on,' he told her, taking another mouthful and chewing it enthusiastically.

Barbara stared fixedly into the blender, her stomach heaving and swirling like the water in the jacuzzi outside.

Matisse watched with reawakened curiosity as Jerry opened more cans and packets and proceeded to concoct a mixture of different brands in a large bowl. Jerry added pepper from the peppermill and gave the mixture a final stir. Then he dipped in the spoon and devoured a whole mouthful.

Jerry's eyes rose to the ceiling in ecstatic approval of the result. 'Excellent!' he exclaimed. 'Now this is real good. One third *Mighty Dog* . . . A third *Kal Kan* liver with some *Puppy Chow* for texture and some *Doggy Dinz Bisk* for crunchiness . . .'

Ignoring Matisse, Jerry set the mountainous bowl of mixed dogfoods on the floor and knelt down on all fours in front of it.

Barbara held onto the edge of the counter and closed her eyes, refusing to believe what she knew she was about to witness.

Jerry bowed his head over the bowl and began to eat. Matisse gaped at him for a few seconds and then bolted over and started to eat with the same ravenous dedication as Jerry.

Barbara tried not to look, yet something compelled her to open her eyes and to watch the bizarre spectacle of man and dog eating side by side on her kitchen floor. But she was not prepared for the sudden convulsive upheaval in her guts when the wholefood sludge in the blender abruptly settled with a furtive belch . . .

# CHAPTER 14

That night Barbara sat at her mirrors slowly massaging avocado and cucumber *purée* into her cheeks and thinking back over the traumatic events of the afternoon. David sat on the bed with his back to her eating a sandwich and half watching the Peter Pan image of Dick Cavet sucking up to one of the British theatrical knights on the TV and half listening to Barbara's incredible account of events.

'I mean . . . I mean he ate the stuff like it was the *pâté maison* from *Maxim's* . . .' she exclaimed after a subdued silence.

David shrugged. 'I told you Barb, the guy has wisdom.'

Barbara checked out her throat for winkles. 'I still don't trust him, Dave.'

'Oh and I gave him the burglar alarm code . . . just in case,' David added, not listening.

Barbara stared at her husband's bare back in the mirror. 'Oh sure, great. Why don't you give the bum a credit card?'

David's ears pricked up. 'Carmen told me she could shop a lot easier if she had the Mastercharge,' he said casually.

Barbara flung her earrings into the jewel box and swung round on her fur-covered stool. 'Maybe Jerry and Carmen could invite us over for dinner one evening,' she rasped, taking a huge swig of her *Screwdriver* and slapping the lid on the pot of face tonic. 'Does the concept *schmuck* mean anything to you Dave?'

David pressed the off button on the remote TV control and slid under the sheet. 'Good night, Barbara,' he forced himself to say.

His wife flounced across the vast white carpet and plonked herself on the bed. 'Good night, David,' she snapped, swigging her tall drink and reaching for the sleep mask hanging on the bedhead.

Her stomach was still feeling extremely queasy.

# CHAPTER 15

Outside in the garden under the indestructible moon, Jerry wandered sleeplessly around in the red Terrycloth bathrobe, breathing in the mingled fragrance of the different fruits and flowers. After a while, he stopped by the laden gratefruit trees and parted the front of the robe. Aiming his cock at an outrageous angle, he peed in a long silver arc, sketching a wavering zigzag pattern down one of the trunks. Matisse appeared from nowhere and watched with rapt attention for a moment. Then he walked up to the tree and copied Jerry at a lower level. Jerry finished his pee, shook his cock and stowed it decently behind the Terrycloth folds. Taking a saved cigarette from a pocket, he lit it and smoked it in short economic puffs in the serenity of the moonlit garden, savouring the luxury of his surroundings, yet glad to be outdoors again under the familiar wide sky.

Matisse trotted over and nuzzled his bare white ankles.

'Hey Matisse, how're ya doin' *amigo*?' Jerry chuckled, wriggling his toes.

The dog scampered away and then returned from the cabana with a squashy rubber ball which he laid at Jerry's feet, wagging his tail expectantly.

'Want to play ball?' Jerry threw the ball a little way and Matisse swiftly retrieved it.

'Let's try a home run . . .' Jerry suggested. He tossed the ball high and far across the patio.

Matisse went after it like a bullet. Leaping high into the air, he crashed unintentionally into the security alarm box on the wall of the pool filtering and pumping system. Immediately the silver silence was ruptured by the oscillating shriek of the sirens.

Max sat bolt upright, instantly awake and with all senses alerted. 'False Alarm. Scene Ninety. Take One . . .' he mumbled, rolling off the futon and grabbing his camera and recorder gear.

In the maid's room, David rolled sideways out from under the galloping Carmen, screwing up his eyes in exquisite agony. 'Jesus Christ . . . I lost another goddam sneeze . . .' he moaned, doubling up over his throbbing crotch and feeling around on the floor for his kimono.

Carmen rolled her eyes ecstatically and lifted her breasts in her hands in expectant bliss. 'Bless you anyway Dave . . .' she gasped.

In the master bedroom, Barbara lay motionless on her back, dead to the world.

Out the front, Jerry and Matisse strolled in the moonlight as if blissfully unaware of the commotion they had caused.

After a while the police helicopter came clattering up from the south, its probing searchlight violating the costly privacy of the secluded empires below. Matisse froze and barked savagely up at the invading machine as it picked out him and Jerry in its relentless glare. Max ran round the corner by the carport, shooting everything in sight with sweeping pans and zooming closeups.

'Just hold it right there, buddy!' shrieked the loud-speaker under the roaring rotors.

'Hold what where?' Jerry asked Matisse with unruffled calm.

The wrought-iron gates at the end of the driveway swung open and two patrol cars screeched up to the house. Two cops jumped out of each one waving guns. One of the cops was dragged across the lawn by the giant German Shepherd.

'Here comes the cavalry,' Jerry grinned.

'Hands over your head!' snapped the cop with the dog.

Matisse fled to his customary refuge under the gleaming cream Rolls Royce.

Jerry reached for the moon.

'What you doin' here?' the cop demanded triumphantly.

Jerry shrugged. 'I just took a piss in the backyard, officer.'

The cop shoved his gun into the suspect's abdomen. 'Let's see some ID,' he snapped.

Jerry shrugged again. 'I don't seem to have any on me.'

Just then David Whiteman came stumbling out of the

front door. 'It's okay, officer . . .' he yelled, waving at Max to get the hell out of it with his recording gear.

The cop prodded Jerry in the belly a second time. 'He's got no identification Mr. Whiteman,' he crowed.

David came between the cop and his grinning house guest. 'He's a bum, officer but he lives here . . . at the moment,' he explained wearily.

The cop sighed with disappointment and holstered his thirty-eight. 'Whatever you say Mr. Whiteman,' he muttered, utterly at a loss.

Lance's little van buzzed through the gates and drew up behind the patrol cars. It was closely followed by Orvis Goodnight wearing a multicoloured polkadot bathrobe and silver slippers.

'What happened this time white man?' Orvis boomed derisively. 'Some nigger vampire set your alarm off?'

'Evening Mr. Goodnight,' David replied with forced civility.

The black record mogul walked right up to his unfortunate neighbour. 'Don't you try to sweet talk me!' he snarled. 'I'm callin' Mayor Bradley and get me some satisfaction.'

Alerted by the proximity of the swaggering black giant to his adopted master, Matisse launched himself at Orvis's silver moccasions.

'I'm gonna sue you for this damn dog!' Orvis yelled, performing a frenetic impromptu tapdance around the dog's snapping jaws.

Jerry ordered Matisse to desist. The dog withdrew instantly to sit at Jerry's feet.

'He is seeing a goddam dog therapist!' David protested.

Orvis grinned horribly. 'I'm gonna send that mutt to dog heaven if he don't stop attacking me and my family . . .' he vowed. 'He just attacks black people, white man. I know you trained him to go for *schwarzes*. And if he craps on my white gravel just one more time I'm gonna nuke his ass!'

With a growl of Doomsday ferocity, Matisse went for the black man's throat. Orvis immediately took to his heels with the raging collie in hot pursuit and leaping crazedl for his buttocks.

'Can we please lose the helicopter?' David pleaded, his head beginning to throb like certain other parts of his anatomy.

One of the cops spoke into his radio and the helicopter dipped forward and departed southwards.

'I think your alarm system still needs a little work,' one of the other cops said grimly as Lance cut off the ear-splitting wail of the sirens.

David gazed up at the bright and ancient face of the moon and sighed. 'Fuck technology . . .' he said.

# CHAPTER 16

One bright morning, when the Californian sun easily eclipsed Santa Claus's rosy grin and the coloured fairy lights adorning his sleigh, David drove Jerry downtown to the Mission Centre. The Mission was situated in a converted warehouse. Though shabby and bleak, the place still provided a semblance of homely security for the hundred or so down and outs, mostly men, lounging listlessly around in chairs, some dozing, others still dazed after a rare night's sleep. In the entrance lobby, a woman was playing a jazz medley with tipsy ecstasy on a backless upright piano set up on a dais of wooden boxes, the smoke from her perpetual cigarette staining a narrow strip of hair a vivid yellow.

Jerry led David up to the reception desk with a certain amount of pride.

'You stay here much?' David asked in a chastened whisper, shocked by the air of desolate loneliness and hopelessness around him.

Jerry shrugged. 'Whenever I'm hard up for clothes or a shower, Dave. Mostly I like to stay out by myself . . .'

They queued up behind three or four ragged figures in front of the cheerless booth. After a few minutes, David wandered away by himself. Hardly anybody was speaking or moving in the vast echoing space. The homeless men sat staring straight ahead and seemed totally unaware of him. He stopped in front of a middle aged balding man and smiled. The man eventually looked up at him and then abruptly looked away. Puzzled and hurt by the brutal rejection of his friendship, David backed away in embarrassment and shame.

A little round man in a baseball cap sidled up to him with an accusing leer. 'You have to wait in line for a number if you want to spend the night . . .' he whined in a sinister undertone.

'It's okay Willie, he's with me,' Jerry called over to him.

Willie nodded and sidled away.

David hurried back to the queue looking shaken. 'That little guy . . . He thought I was a . . . That I was looking for a bed!' he murmured to Jerry.

Jerry grinned. 'Or a meal. The food here's pretty good, Dave. No cream cheese and banana though.'

Or *Puppy Chow* David was tempted to add, remembering what Barbara had told him several nights previously.

Jerry shuffled forward as the line moved up.

The clerk behind the desk obviously knew him well. 'Hey Jerry, I got your packet here,' he said, holding up a brown paper parcel. 'You checking in for a while?'

'No Barry. Do I have any mail?' Jerry asked in mock seriousness.

The clerk squinted at the pigeon holes. 'Book of the Month Club . . .' he joked, shaking his head.

Jerry took the package. 'Well, thanks for holding this for me anyway.'

Barry eyed his old acquaintance appraisingly. 'Hey Jerry, you look pretty sharp,' he exclaimed, much impressed by the new image. He leaned over the desk confidentially. 'Did you hear about Red Turner? He caught a cab . . .'

Jerry shrugged sadly and patted the clerk's arm. 'Next time Barry . . .' he said cryptically.

Jerry led David away, leaving another bum to take his place at the desk with depressing inevitability.

Outside in the parking lot, David looked utterly disheartened as he unlocked the Rolls. 'I don't understand how you can take that kind of life Jerry,' he mumbled. 'It's such a downer.'

Jerry looked surprised. 'But Dave, the Mission is the best part of it,' he claimed.

David waved the car keys. 'You got your licence?'

'Yep. Sure have.'

David handed him the keyes. 'Okay Jerry, there you go. You drive.'

Jerry grabbed the keys with bright-eyed eagerness, like a kid with a new toy.

They got in and Jerry backed carefully out of the space. 'Where to, Boss?' he grinned.

David looked totally at a loss. 'Don't know. Some days you just . . . you just want to take off . . . just go anywhere . . .' he said vaguely, as though suddenly bereft of all initiative after visiting the Mission.

Jerry looked as if he understood exactly. 'Okay, let's hit the beach,' he suggested, accelerating out into the traffic. 'I got some good friends down there.'

They had been driving for some time when David suddenly frowned and stared around him as if he had just awakened out of a drugged sleep. 'Hey wait a minute! My business . . . Who'll pay the bills?' he demanded, shocked at his momentary fit of irresponsibility.

'You're putting me on Dave,' Jerry laughed.

'You know what I spend a *month*?' David exclaimed.

Jerry turned onto Santa Monica. 'Horseshit!' he scoffed. 'You got enough dough for ten lifetimes.'

David opened his mouth to order Jerry to head for the DAVE-BAR plant. But then he shut it again and relaxed into the passenger seat, letting the breeze and the sunshine play on his face through the open sunroof. 'Maybe *I* should be a bum,' he sighed. 'No more bills, no more hangers, no more problems . . .'

'You wouldn't last five minutes, Dave.'

David rose to the challenge. 'Okay, the beach. Let's hit it *pronto*!' he ordered.


The Venice Beach walkway was not crowded, despite the flawless blue sky with just a trace of haze over the Los Angeles urban sprawl. A few cyclists weaved lazily in and out of the casual strollers with their pulsing Walkmans, old folk sat and gazed at the ocean and perhaps the past, and rollerskaters threaded skilfully among the obstacles with effortless ease. David and Jerry ambled slowly along eating giant slices of pizza. David Whiteman looked happier and more relaxed than he had for a long time. He'd taken off his jacket and his tie and rolled up his shirtsleeves. He drank in the fresh sea breeze and the sunshine and allowed Jerry to guide him around his familiar haunts.

They passed a black man of about fifty with grey tinges to his curly black hair, who was sitting on a ledge next to an old dog also going grey at the edges. Between them, a prehistoric transistor radio was blaring out Ravel's *Bolero*. Further along under some palms, a tall turbanned man in jogging shorts was giving a girl a neck message, while beside them a punk hippy was playing a battered guitar connected to a small amplifier. A brown girl in a bikini rollerskated round and round a small patio area, watched by a dozen or so leathery bums sitting or lying and drinking on flaking wooden benches.

'Looks just like the sixties . . .' David muttered, as if dredging up the images from his early twenties.

Jerry smiled. 'That's the beach for you.' Suddenly he caught sight of somebody he recognised among the boozing hobos on the benches. 'Hey, Tom Tom . . .!' he yelled with delight, rushing over to an old Red Indian wino wearing plaits and a bowler hat.

Tom Tom was already well away, drinking with reckless abandon from a litre bottle of *rosé*, but he slapped hands with Jerry and chuckled throatily. 'Hey, you're looking fancy, Professor!' he growled, his dulled eyes briefly lighting up with pleasure.

Jerry introduced David.

'Pleased to meet you Tom Tom,' Dave smiled, fascinated and moved by the old Indian's simple affection for Jerry.

'You want a drink, white man?' Tom Tom offered him the bottle.

David hesitated, suddenly disconcerted. 'How'd you know my name?' he asked in amazement.

Tom Tom chuckled and winked at Jerry. 'Hey Dave, say hallo to Ed here and my good buddy on the guitar Patrick, and this here is Dorothy.' He waved at his three younger companions.

Patrick, a grizzled redneck, was picking chords on a guitar with huge fingers. Dorothy looked young enough to be David's daughter. Barefoot and wearing only jeans and a tanktop, she looked very pretty beneath the grime and the needle marks.

David nodded and smiled. He found it hard to speak. 'How do you do?' he finally managed to ask Dorothy.

'I do fine Dave . . . How do you do?' she said, swigging from her bottle of Martini.

David had to look away. 'Tom Tom . . . Is that your real name?' he asked the old Indian.

'Hell no! My real name is Harold Whitefeather,' Tom Tom chuckled, taking a swig of *rosé* before passing the half-empty bottle across to Jerry with another wink.

'Whitefeather . . . That's a really beautiful name,' David said awkwardly.

Tom Tom nodded. 'My Indian name is . . .' He uttered a string of Indian words. 'It means He Who Runs With The Speed Of The Deer.'

Ed, a skinny crewcut Vietnam veteran of about thirty, pointed at Tom Tom's gnarled frame and giggled helplessly.

Jerry passed the bottle to David. David took out his handkerchief to wipe the top clean, but then he thought better of it. He raised the bottle in silent but heartfelt tribute to the four bums and to Jerry, and then took a long drink of the sweet pink liquid, conscious of Tom Tom's wise eyes boring into him. Wiping his mouth, he sat down next to Patrick who immediately began to sing *See The Pyramids Along The Nile* in a surprisingly gentle and sensitive voice, strumming subtle chords in accompaniment.

Tears sprang out of Ed's vacant eyes. David sat back among his new friends, touched by the young veteran's hopeless unspoken grief, and took another long cool swig of the acid wine.

Late that night the phone rang in the Whiteman residence, shattering the brittle silence that had prevailed all evening in the luxurious living-room where Barbara and Carmen sat staring unseeingly at the television. They both leaped up together and scrambled across the room to answer it.

Barbara got there first. 'Hallo . . . Hallo . . . Dave? Are you all right?' she shouted hoarsely when she heard his slurred voice at the other end. 'What the hell happened to you? I called the factory, I called your parents, I called Sidney, I called the police . . .'

Carmen stood watching her mistress's face gradually

harden from hysterical anxiety into contempt and pale anger.

'You're spending the night with Jerry . . . at the beach . . .?' Barbara echoed incredulously. 'Dave, are you drunk?'

She listened while David explained that everything was all right and that he was with Jerry and Tom Tom and Ed and Patrick and Dorothy.

'Dorothy who?' she demanded frostily.

Her husband muttered a few incoherent phrases of explanation and then said, 'See ya *mañana* honey . . .' and hung up.

Barbara stared at the receiver for a while and then slowly replaced it. 'I knew that bum was big trouble . . .' she seethed through her perfect white teeth, marching back to the sofa and draining her tall *Screwdriver* in a single gulp.

Carmen's gypsy eyes flashed with jealousy and suspicion. 'Is Dave . . . Señor Dave . . . Is he okay?' she asked, correcting herself hastily.

Barbara nodded abstractedly and muttered something inaudible.

Carmen stood near the phone wringing her hands and biting her lip, until finally she could bear the suspense no longer. She stepped forward boldly. 'Who is this Dorothy?' she blurted out, curling her lip and tossing back her head like a flamenco dancer.

Barbara shook her head and held out her empty glass for a refill. 'That's just what *I* want to know . . .' she muttered menacingly.


David hung up the payphone and strolled past the floodlit weight-lifting arena at the edge of the beach, where a teenage Hercules in tiny gold posing trunks was performing endless pushups between two bollards with a couple of laughing girls sitting astride his back and drinking Coca Cola through straws. Two or three other young muscleheads were sitting around yelling encouragement. David blinked and shook his alcohol-befuddled head at the bizarre rodeo and then wandered onto the sand toards the huddle of drunken transients clustered around the remains of a large driftwood fire.

Tom Tom, Patrick, Ed and Dorothy were fast asleep cocooned in bedrolls and a variety of castoff blankets, but Jerry was sitting staring at the white line of surf along the shore and smoking a cigarette. David kicked the glowing embers closer together to concentrate the last of the blaze and settled down with his jacket round his shoulders to muse about the extraordinary diversity of people addicted to the outdoors life.

'How long you been diddling Carmen?'

David was abruptly jerked out of his reverie. He stared at Jerry's twinkling eyes in the firelight. 'What're you talking about?' he murmured, taken completely unaware.

Jerry nudged him gently. 'Hey, it's all right by me,' he assured him almost in admiration. 'She's a hot little *frijolita* . . . And Barbara, now she's a handsome lady too.'

David shrugged guiltily. 'Look Jerry, I've been married to Barb for a long time now . . . And Carmen's cute and she's hot and there it is . . . You ever been married?'

His friend nodded. 'Twice.'

David stared into the fire. 'Well, you get into the horse latitudes every once in a while . . . You hit a dead calm and you have to juice things up a bit . . .' He trailed off shamefacedly.

'A little hot sauce,' Jerry agreed.

David was quiet for a while. 'I mean, I think Barbara should have a fling too. I think it would get her going again,' he said earnestly, glancing up at the moon. 'I do love her you know.'

'Yes I believe you do, Dave.'

They watched the surf for a time.

'Were you really married twice?' David asked eventually.

'Naw Dave, I was just kidding.'

'Were you really a writer and an actor?'

Jerry's face looked oddly innocent in the flickering firelight. He glanced round at their sleeping companions and his face grew graver, but still bright with lively wonder. 'What a piece of work is a man . . .!' he murmured. 'How noble in reason! How infinite in faculty! In form and moving how express and admirable! In action how like an angel! In apprehension how like a god! The beauty of the world! The paragon of animals!'

Struck dumb by the unexpected power and understanding in Jerry's musical voice, David sat and gaped at him in awed respect.

Jerry paused and pulled a wry face, meeting David's gaze with ironically sparkling eyes. He picked up a handful of white sand and let it slowly trickle from his fingers in a silvery stream in the moonlight. 'And yet, to me, what is this quintessence of dust . . .?'

Jerry's speech died away amid the sound of the waves and the two friends sat watching the pictures in the embers until at last they both fell asleep propped against each other.

# CHAPTER 17

Next morning they drove along the boulevards under the leaping reindeer and the puffing hearty cheeks of the Santa Clauses, their clothes rumpled and grimy and their faces haggard but happy.

Eventually Jerry turned into the Whitemans' driveway just as Orvis Goodnight was pulling out of his gates. The music mogul frowned through his tinted windscreen at the dishevelled duo in the front of the other cream Rolls Royce.

'Goddamit, there goes the neighbourhood!' Orvis exclaimed with a shudder, braking to watch his neighbour clamber wearily out of his car with his crumpled jacket slung over his shoulder. Then he switched on his stereo full blast and accelerated away down the hill.

Just as David and Jerry entered the house, a tour bus slowed by the gates and a woman in a floral dress with blue hair and diamante upswept spectacles craned out of the window. 'Hey, isn't that Starsky and Hutch!' she screamed in ecstasy.

Jerry turned in the doorway and gave her the prongs.

With squeals of outraged delight from the sightseeing matrons, the bus rumbled on its way uphill.

The two buddies met Barbara emerging from the bedroom into the hallway at the same time as Carmen and Max wielding his video gear appeared along the passage from the kitchen.

'I will never ever forgive you,' Barbara declared in a choked voice, twisting her long strings of pearls as if preparing a garrote with which to strangle both returning prodigals. She pointed at Jerry. 'That disgusting derelict is responsible and you both stink to high heaven.'

David tried to take her hands. 'Barb, I spent the night with some poor oppressed fellow human beings,' he told her happily, his eyes clear and bright despite lack of proper sleep. He twitched a piece of seaweed out of his hair. 'They live like animals, but they still possess the capacity for joy.'

His wife's crimson lips trembled querulously. 'I was panic-stricken, David. You had no right to put me through that.'

He smiled with weary patience. 'I ate garbage last night Barb and I loved it,' he revealed.

'Great. Then you can have garbage tonight for dinner!' Barbara promised, glancing at Carmen.

But her anger and sarcasm seemed totally lost on her quietly smiling husband. He stood there gazing back at her like a born again convert. 'I learned to beg Barbara,' he confessed proudly. 'This morning some guy . . . a total stranger . . . he gave me two quarters.'

Jerry slipped off a shoe and tipped sand out onto the polished hall floor watched by the outraged maid and the outraged Barbara. 'Think I'll take and shower and grab some breakfast,' he announced calmly, moving off towards one of the bathrooms.

Barbara threw up her hands and her breasts followed, heaving and wobbling with indignation inside the open knit sweater. 'You're pushing me to my limits . . . Both of you!' she cried, storming back into the bedroom.

Max zoomed in on his father's puzzled face. 'Return of Superhanger . . . End of Scene One,' he muttered.

# CHAPTER 18

Later that morning, after David had cleaned himself up and changed and driven off to the DAVE-BAR factory, Barbara drew back the drapes across the bedroom patio windows and sat on the bed clutching the telephone and staring fixedly at the transistor radio on her dressing table. She was listening both to the telephone and to the voice of Dr. Toni Grant chattering huskily out of the radio.

' . . . there's just no way to justify incest,' Toni was telling her menopausal, housebound audience. 'And now let's try to get one more call before the break . . . One more call now . . . Hallo . . .?'

Barbara galvanised herself into action. 'Hallo Dr. Grant . . . My name is . . . my name is Dawn and I'm . . . I'm twenty six years old and I live in . . . in Toluca Lake . . .'

'We have Dawn on the line,' Toni Grant announced flatly from the speaker. 'Dawn from Toluca Lake . . . Hallo there, Dawn . . .'

Barbara gripped the phone nervously and kept her eyes glued to the radio. 'Dr. Grant . . . I'm a wreck . . . a nervous wreck . . .' she confessed. 'My husband has recently brought this bum home to live with us and I'm feeling . . .'

The radio agony counsellor interrupted her brusquely. 'Yes of course you are Dawn, of course you are. That's perfectly understandable, it sounds like you do have a genuine problem . . . At least your husband does. Is your husband a happy man, Dawn . . .?'

'Not lately . . .' Barbara heard herself saying out of the radio after the disconcerting few seconds transmission delay.

'Well now, Dawn . . .' Dr. Toni breezed on. 'It's possible your husband's vicariously living a freer life through the close presence of this street person he's brought into your household.'

'I'm very depressed, Dr. Grant,' Barbara heard her voice admit from the radio.

'How's your sex life?' Dr. Grant inquired, as if she were asking about a house plant.

'Non-existent at the moment,' said Barbara's voice hoarsly.

'We have to take a commercial break . . .' the radio informed her. 'Can you hold, Dawn?'

Barbara hesitated. At that moment the front door bell chimed hideously.

Jerry answered the door munching a tuna-on-rye sandwich.

A well-heeled Beverly Hills matron was standing on the thresh-old brandishing a pledge clipboard. 'Mr. Whiteman, we're collecting money to help the starving in Ethiopia,' she announced automatically.

Jerry wiped his mouth. 'Put me down for a thousand dollars . . .' he said lazily and shut the door on her.

The woman stood rooted to the spot thanking the front door. 'That's very nice of you Mr. Whiteman,' she exclaimed. 'Have a nice decade.'

David Whiteman himself was sitting in a traffic jam on La Cienaga with sweat pouring down under his tight collar as he listened to the car radio with incredulous panic. During the commercial break he mopped his pale face and neck and steeled himself to hear the rest of his wife's treacherous interview on the phone-in show. But Barbara never came back on the line. There was no response to Dr. Toni Grant's teeth 'n' smiles intro to the second half of her programme. A crazy idea crossed David's mind and he leaned over and dialled the station's phone-in number on the car phone. The instant he got through, he prayed that the jam would ease and force him to abandon his plan. Next moment he was on the air.

'Hallo . . . Dr. Grant . . . Hallo . . .?' he said, pinching his nose with his free hand. 'My name is Bob and I'm twenty seven years old and I'm no longer attracted to my wife and this bothers me . . .' He dried up and sat helpless in the fouled up traffic.

Toni Grant's husky response made him jump. 'How long has this situation been going on, Bob?'

Suddenly the traffic lane ahead began to move. David eased forward, steering with his elbows. 'About nine and a half years,' he replied after thinking quickly.

The traffic ahead suddenly stopped dead. David stamped on the brake. Next moment there was a mighty crunch from behind as something rammed the Rolls in the rear.

'As long as that, Bob?'

'You dirty sonofabitch!' David's normal voice suddenly blared out of the radio.

'Now I'm only trying to help you Bob . . .' Toni Grant scolded him out of the speakers. 'But your anger and frustration are perfectly understandable. After all . . .'

David slammed the receiver down and opened his door to confront the driver of the vehicle behind. When he saw who it was, he groaned in dismay and sank back into his seat dabbing the sweat from his brow.

# CHAPTER 19

Barbara's nerve had failed at the last minute and she had hung up on Dr. Toni Grant before the end of the commercial break. She was now out on the patio awaiting the demonstration of the new miniature waterfall that her landscape specialist – Geraldo – had created for the planned Japanese patio.

Geraldo cane tripping across from the water control apparatus in the filtering unit, his willowy body trembling with excitement. 'Now my dear, we want this little cataract to make a statement . . .' he purred, adjusting his *Cage Aux Folles* hat and squinting at the delicate little feature he had constructed at the edge of the lawn.

There was a series of hisses and gurgles from under the paving and then a needle-sharp jet of water spurted out of one of the tiny holes among the white stones and hit Barbara smack in the eye. She tottered backwards with a scream and all but fell into the pool, saved only by the handrail alongside the ladder.

On the other side of the patio, Max broke up with laughter and zoomed in to capture his mother's reaction on tape.

Barbara looked ready to commit homicide as Geraldo fussed around her with a pink and lavender spotted handkerchief. 'Well my dear, it's not Niagara Falls . . .' he pouted, dabbing at his client's eye. 'But there are bound to be teething troubles, *n'est ce pas?*'

Barbara brushed the popinjay aside with a sweep of her brawny arm. 'You'll be the one with teething troubles,' she muttered, resisting the temptation to pick up a white pebble and ram it down his throat.

Nigel, the dungareed pipefitter, ducked out of the filter housing. 'You'll have to replace these valves. They're at least twenty years old,' he informed her. 'It'll cost between three and eight thousand.'

But Barbara had stopped listening. She was advancing round the pool towards Max with his video gear, glaring at his expensive camera with murderous intent. Max started to back away, still recording, but unsure what his mother might do.

She came right up to him and leaned forward, thrusting her big face right into the inscrutable darkness of the lens. 'Stop it Max . . .! Stop it . . .!' she yelled hysterically. 'My centre is coming apart. It really is, Max. I need your help. I really do. This is my second breakdown in only one year.' Her shoulders began to heave under her expensive woollen shirt, making the strings of pearls rattle like bones in some obscure native ritual dance. Tears began to pour down her face and she bowed her head in abject humiliation.

Max switched off the camera and quietly put down the video gear on a nearby lounger. Then he put his arms tenderly around his mother and held her tightly against him while she sobbed her heart out on his shoulder.

With a piercing whistle, the rest of the waterfall outlets abruptly burst into life and sprayed everyone with a drenching broadside of stinging water . . .

# CHAPTER 20

Across the velvet lawn under the fragrant fruit trees Jerry
Baskins was performing an elaborate routine of *Tai Chi*
exercises clad in a sort of loincloth he had fashioned from
an old teeshirt. Nearby, Matisse lay in the shade with his
head on his paws watching with mystified awe. From his
bedroom window, Max was gazing at the mysterious balletic
movements and gestures with rapt attention, all thought of
desecrating the ancient ceremonial by video recording it
banished firmly from his mind. Carmen was also at her
window concealed behind the slatted blind, her forgotten
cigarette burning down to a long tube of unbroken ash
between her fingers. Barbara too was a captivated spectator
behind the half-drawn net drapes in her bedroom. She had
taken off her pink slacks and was standing just in the shirt
which came down to her knees and which she had opened
almost all the way, so that her magificent breasts swelled
awesomely against the window. She pressed a hot towel to
her forehead and stared through her sunglasses at the
graceful and sensuous dance the hated interloper was
performing with enviably effortless ease, and her full red
lips parted in reverent wonder.

After a while Jerry noticed her tall statuesque figure in
the shadows and particularly her thrusting breasts just
caught by the rays of the sinking sun. He stopped his
exercises and shaded his eyes. 'Another headache, Barbara?'
he called with genuine concern.

Barbara was startled, believing herself to be invisible.
She moved to the opening in the glass shutters. 'Oh, it's
chronic,' she replied awkwardly, patting the hot towel with
long suffering resignation. 'Jerry, where did you learn to
do that stuff?' she asked shyly.

'The *Tai Chi*? In an *ashram* in Oregon.'

Barbara slid the patio door further open. 'You were in

an *ashram* Jerry? Her voice was breathy and had lost its edge.

Jerry took a few steps towards the house. 'Maybe I could do something to help your headache,' he suggested.

Barbara uttered the short sharp laugh of the long suffering martyr. 'Oh I doubt it Jerry . . .' she smiled wanly, massaging the towel against her forehead with sensuous intensity and throwing back her head so that her breasts pushed even harder against the glass.

Without another word Jerry wandered casually into the house. Intrigued, Matisse got to his feet and loped after him like a devoted slave.

Barbara found herself flinging her hot towel into a corner and drawing the net curtains fully closed. The white bedroom was bathed in a soft, seductive golden light. She sat on the corner of the bed and listened to her heart hammering with fearful expectation.

A couple of minutes later, Jerry came in and closed the door and walked barefoot over the fluffy carpet towards her.

'At the *ashram* we learned a Balinese massage technique that's really powerful,' he said quietly.

Barbara laughed nervously. 'I don't know, Jerry. I'm a little . . . I'm a little tense,' she murmured.

He put his hands on her shoulders. 'I'd say you were rigid as a racquet,' he said, ever so slightly pushing the collar of the shirt aside and exposing more of her firm brown flesh.

Barbara closed her eyes, flinching lightly at his touch. 'I'm very angry with you and I'm pissed at Dave for going off with you,' she told him in a far from angry tone.

Jerry gradually began to massage her shoulders and neck with slow, supple hands. His touch was gentle but also strong.

'I had acupuncture, but it didn't help,' Barbara revealed.

'Wrong *karma*,' Jerry declared flatly, pushing the shirt almost off her shoulders. 'You see Barbara, headaches are mostly related to built-up anxiety and tension . . .'

The shirt slipped off her shoulders and gathered around

her waist. Barbara gasped and gave an involuntary shudder as her body was unveiled.

'Lie down,' Jerry commanded.

After the briefest hesitation Barbara obeyed meekly.

'You have to find a way to release the tension,' Jerry explained softly.

Barbara rolled her legs up onto the bed and lay on her side. 'It's very difficult for me to release my anxiety . . .' she confessed, with a trace of challenge in her voice.

'Of course it is,' Jerry murmured, deftly removing the shirt and casting it over his shoulder. He turned her onto her stomach and rubbed his hands together to warm them. 'Now don't be afraid, Barbara. I'm going to use my aura . . .'

Jerry commenced a thorough massage of Barbara's entire body, his strong hands flitting over her blooming skin and scarcely touching it.

Barbara shuddered again. The lightness of his touch and yet the firmness of his aura was unbearably arousing. 'I'm still afraid . . .' she admitted as he gave her back and hips a wonderful *effleurage*.

'Just relax,' he whispered, setting up a strong wavelike rhythm as he moulded her back and thighs and buttocks with skilful caresses.

Barbara began to writhe and moan. She had not been handled that way for years and the experience was both a thrill and a profound shock to her. 'Oh! Oh! Oh! Oh! . . . Sorry . . . Sorry . . .' she gasped, biting into the pillows.

'Your body is letting go, all the tensions are seeping out through my hands . . .' Jerry murmured, flipping her over onto her back.

Crouching in the bedside rug, Matisse clamped his jaws round a mouthful of thick woollen pile and panted in time with Jerry's movements and the tides of Barbara's rising passion.

'I can really *feel* it . . .!' Barbara gasped.

Matisse whined into the rug as if to say 'So can I.'

'The headache?' Jerry asked, rubbing his palms round and round on Barbar's huge red nipples.

'Fading . . . Fading . . .' she moaned, swinging her

heavy hips in ever-increasing gyrations, her eyes fixed on the unmistakable stirrings beneath Jerry's improvised loincloth. 'I think . . . I think I see your aura . . .' she panted.

'Well, I sure as hell can feel it . . .' Jerry breathed, moving down and stroking her feet and her legs with long elaborate movements. 'You have great skin Barbara . . .'

She closed her eyes and rolled her head from side to side in the opposite direction to her hips. 'Thank you Jerry . . . I'm so relaxed . . . So relaxed . . .' she cried, cupping her breasts and squeezing them in time with his manipulations.

In the white undergrowth of the rug, Matisse was tearing feverishly at the pile and yelping with increasing excitement.

Suddenly Barbara burst into huge shuddering sobs, smiling and weeping at the same time. 'Jerry!' she howled. 'Something strange is happening . . . I'm scared . . .'

Jerry moved his hands up to her hips again. 'You're just freeing up. Let yourself go,' he urged. 'Let it all happen.'

Arching her body with greedy abandon, Barbara flung her arms round his neck and pulled him on top of her. The loincloth finally gave way under the strain and burst asunder. Clasped tightly together, they slid off the low bed and onto the rug. Matisse slunk away under the dressing table and clamped his teeth round a slipper, stifling the urge to bay like the Baskerville Hound at the prospect of another victim crossing the misty moors.

'Take me Jerry . . . Invade me . . . Jangle me . . . I need it . . . Don't stop now . . . Don't deny me . . .' Barbara cried, devouring his lips and digging her scarlet nails into his sweating back.

Suddenly a piercing scream rent the air as Jerry thrust powerfully into her, transformed abruptly from the caressing masseur into the road-drilling bull.

'Yes! Yes! Yes!' Barbara cried as Jerry gave her the works, his glistening body ramming back and forth like a well-oiled machine.

The climax eventually came with a primeval scream from Barbara that seemed to tear through the house and reverberate all over Beverly Hills.

Mr. Nagamichi paused in his hedge clipping and stared

up into the evening sky, uncertain what he had heard. In the kitchen, Carmen stopped mopping the tiled floor and stared at the doorway in disbelief. On the patio the new waterfall burst devastatingly into life again, drenching the windows of the house with torrents of water. Birds rose in clouds from the trees and the jacuzzi bubbled like a hot spring. Up on the scaffolding around the Masouds' new minaret, a young workman glanced down at the Whitemans' roof with envious lust. Matisse ran out into the garden and began to howl like a banshee. Soon Orvis Goodnight's Afghans had taken up the refrain, and it quickly spread around the neighbourhood in a chorus of vicarious canine ecstasy.

Barbara lay back on the pillows smoking a cigarette without inhaling. 'I haven't had an orgasm like that in . . . in nine and a half years,' she eventually murmured in serene and blissful relaxation. 'I'm ashamed of myself. I never dreamed I was capable of this. I'm glad, Jerry, glad and ashamed. Exhausted and invigorated at the same time.' She turned to the trembling, sweating figure lying beside her staring at the ceiling. 'Just as I was repelled and yet attracted to you at the same time, Jerry. It's *Yin* and *Yang* isn't it?'

Jerry looked ravaged and utterly drained. 'It was just one of those things,' he muttered.

Barbara was bursting with new vitality and confidence. She finished her cigarette and stubbed it out in an empty tumbler. 'Dave lost interest in me and I lost interest in sex,' she said. 'I shopped for gratification . . . Compulsively. I bought dogfood . . . and that's sex without a climax.' She snuggled against him. 'All that meditation and all that yoga never got me to this place.' She fell silent for a moment. 'You know I'm perfectly well aware of Dave and sweet Carmen . . . I mean, I felt he needed a little confidence building and I thought maybe she might be able to invigorate him for me. But of course I was denying myself and all the desire was building up in me like a volcano . . .' She stroked Jerry's hairy abdomen. 'And you unleashed it for me Jerry and I'm glad to be back in the real world again.'

Barbara opened her eyes and gazed at the photograph of

her husband on the dressing table. 'Poor Dave, he's such a passionate man, a sweet man, Jerry . . . But you . . . It was you who found my . . .' She closed her eyes again, reliving the previous hour. 'This was a one time trip to the moon Jerry. It happened and there's nothing we can do about it now, no matter how fantastic it was.' She rolled over and smothered his face between her breasts. 'We can never ever repeat this adventure. Never . . .'

There was silence for a long time. Then Jerry stirred slightly. 'I agree Barbara,' he said in a muffled sleepy voice. He didn't really have any choice.

A little later, Jerry got up and wandered hazily out to the bathroom. He pushed open the unlocked door and froze in his tracks, open-mouthed with astonishment. Reflected in the mirror covering most of the wall above the washbasin was a half naked Max, his red hair in curlers, putting the finishing touches to a garnish, almost operatic eye makeup. Jerry stared at the boy's clown mouth outlined in a deep Revlon red. Max stared back at the intruder, shocked and suprised, but not furtive or guilty.

Jerry frowned and then smiled faintly. 'Max, I think you should go with something a little more orange,' he advised.

They looked at one another for a moment and Max's eyes betrayed a kind of grateful relief, as if at long last some terrible taboo had forever been broken. He smiled and nodded. Jerry also nodded and then quietly slipped out of the bathroom, leaving the confused teenager to confront his new liberated self in the giant mirror.

# CHAPTER 21

Just before darkness fell a Police Department towtruck drew up at the gates. David Whiteman got out and staggered wearily up the driveway staring straight ahead of him with a sullen and dangerous look. Next door Mr. Masoud was ushering five chadoored women into his stretched Mercedes limousine. The Iranian caught sight of Jerry Baskins teaching Matisse some new tricks under the trees on the front lawn and wandered across to the fence diving the two properties.

'Thank you for speaking to my son Akbar,' Masoud said, bowing slightly in his immaculate business suit. 'Akbar is very lonely here in Beverly Hills. He has few friends.'

Jerryy smiled amiably and shrugged off the matter with a modest shake of the head.

David stopped as he was about to enter the house and watched the Iranian peel five hundred dollars off the fat wad of twenties in his pocket and offer them to Jerry.

'Perhaps Akbar could visit you one day for Coke and backgammon?' Mr. Masoud ventured to suggest.

Jerry walked rapidly over to the fence and took the generous reward before the Iranian could change his mind. 'Oh sure, any time at all . . .' he mumbled, stunned at his good fortune.

Mr. Masoud bowed again. 'Thank you once more sir,' he said courteously and walked back to his car.

Jerry stood clutching the money and the fence, gaping as the ostentatious limousine wafted out onto the road and disappeared down the hill.

Rubbing his eyes in disbelief, David stumbled into the kitchen where Barbara, looking perky and relaxed in a lemon trouser suit, was blending her dinner in the whirring liquidiser.

'Jesus, what a day!' he muttered, leaning on the counter as if he'd just run a marathon. 'A goddam cop car smashed into the back of the Rolls and now the Iranian guy next door just gave Jerry five hundred dollars for saying hallo to his son.'

Barbara switched off the blender and smiler sweetly. 'You look tired darling,' she cooed. 'Can I fix you a drink?'

David stared at her in disgust. 'I know that wouldn't last you an afternoon at Saks but to some people that's a lot of money,' he snapped.

Barbara went to the refrigerator and mixed him a drink. 'Rum, low calorie tonic, slice of lime . . .' she intoned like a bartender taking an order.

David took the drink and sipped sullenly. 'Thanks Barb,' he said eventually. 'Sorry I snarled. I guess I'm just a bit tense at the moment.'

Barbara mixed herself a *Screwdriver*. 'That's okay darling. Oh, a man from the Municipal Authority came by today and said we had Norwegian rats. It's an epidemic or something.'

Her husband peered morosely into his drink. 'I'm sure glad they're Norwegian. They're probably building a ski jump on the patio.'

Barbara giggled and sipped her *Screwdriver*. 'Maybe they just want some herring.'

David looked up sharply, frowning with anxiety. 'Since when did you start drinking again?' he demanded.

Barbara shrugged. 'I'm a vegetarian Dave, remember? So Vodka comes from a berry doesn't it?' She moved over to him and flung her arms around his neck. Then she gave him a big wet kiss.

Carmen, who just happened to be passing the doorway, stopped and glared at David with resentful hatred. Unseen by Barbara, he tried to signal that he was helpless in her powerful embrace.

'I'm crazy for you Dave, real crazy. . . .' Barbara told him, nibbling his ear and his neck. 'Come on, do it to me. Do it to me sweetie. Make me come fifty-five times.'

Choking with jealous anger, Carmen stifled a shriek and ran to her room in a flood of hot tears.

# CHAPTER 22

Barbara lay in the arms of Morpheus with a smile of blissful serenity on her avocadoed and cucumbered face. She had not bothered with the eye mask, for sleep seemed to have embraced her very readily that night. The silk sheet lay rumpled around her thighs, revealing a set of very scanty and very frilly lingrie. Her husband lay tossing sleeplessly beside her, the eye mask over his face, his body tense and rigid. His head was aching fit to burst.

After hours of futile agony, he ripped off the mask and got out of bed in exasperation. Throwing on his kimono, he padded cautiously into the kitchen without switching on the fluorescent overhead light. He heard Matisse growl and immediately kicked out savagely. 'Don't you fuck with me or I'll nuke your balls you mutt!' he snarled.

To his surprise and relief the dog stopped growling and slunk away under the counter.

David went towards the fridge and then stopped and listened. He heard voices and suppressed laughter coming from Carmen's room just along the passage. Carmen sighed and giggled and then Jerry's gutteral voice murmured something indistinctly. Weak-kneed with jealousy, David crept along the passage toward's the maid's door. With a guilty hollow feeling in his stomach, he bent down to peek through' the keyhole. Just before his eye met the bright yellow little opening, he managed to stop himself. Deafeated, he straightened up and retrated shamefacedly back to the kitchen.

The voices began again, as if in cruel mockery. 'Oh Jerry . . . *Si* . . . *Lo me gusta mucho* . . .' Carmen cried tremulously.

'Calm down *chiquita* . . .' grunted Jerry.

'Oh, but Jerry I love that . . . I love it! Do it again!'

David gripped the handle of the refrigerator door as if he were about to hurl it bodily through the window.

'They always said you Latins were excitable,' Jerry exclaimed breathelessly.

'Oh yes . . . Oh yes . . .!' Carmen almost screamed.

Boiling with impotent rage, David started opening and shutting cupboard doors and rattling cutlery, determined to put a stop to the outrageous activities going on next door. But his tactics only provoked gales of laughter from Carmen's room. David picked up a heavy saucepan and dropped it on the floor. Instantly the laughter and muffled chatter grew louder and more mocking. He turned on the blender and its raucous whine filled the house. But the derisive laughter simply increased the more noise he made. David strode around the kitchen bagning and kicking things and imagining all manner of erotic horseplay going on in Carmen's room.

Eventually he acknowledged that he was in a no-win situation. He opened the fridge in search of something to eat to stifle his jealous fury.

Next moment Jerry walked in wearing the Terrycloth bathrobe. He switched on the light and picked up the saucepan and odd items of cutlery scattered over the floor. Then he turned off the blender.

David kept his head buried in the fridge. 'Jerry, did you just diddle Carmen?' he asked in a menacing udertone.

'Yes Dave, I did.'

'Why?'

'Well Dave, she asked me to fix her TV. Next thing I know she's all over me,' Jerry explained simply.

'You're a bastard,' David told him.

They heard Carmen's door open. 'Jerry, bring me a Tab please,' she called without attempting to lower her voice.

Jerry smiled sadly. 'Well, I guess it's time for me to go,' he sighed. 'So long Dave.'

David slammed the fridge door and swung round. 'You can stay Jerry, but never play around with my maid again!' he rapped, his eyes hard with a steely glint that Jerry had not seen before. He took a vicious bite out of the enormous banana he was holding and strode threateningly out of the kitchen.

Matisse growled halfheartedly and watched Jerry take a couple of cans of Tab out of the fridge.

If dogs smile, Matisse was smiling.

# CHAPTER 23

Next morning David sat on the sofa in the living-room tying his necktie and watching Max's latest video message to him on the TV. His eyes were sunken from lack of sleep and he kept yawning, his mouth gaping like a hippopotamus's. He was very late for work.

On the screen Max was standing in front of a moped store flanked by rows of gleaming bikes on the forecourt. 'Dad, could I please have a moped . . .?' he was pleading directly into the camera with disconcerting frankness. 'It's chsaper than the car and I promise I'll wear a helmet all the time. Also, if you don't get me a moped I'll kill myself . . .'

Max vanished out of frame and the camera zoomed in on the price tag of a deluxe model fitted with all the latest accessories and refinements. The image lingered for a while and then the screen went blank.

With a groan David got up and wandered out towards the patio, ripping off the bungled tie and starting all over again.

Outside Barbara was sitting in a deckchair reading a Gore Vidal novel. Nearby, Carmen was seated at the edge of the pool shelling peas and thinking about the night before. In the pool Jerry was teaching Mattisse some new tricks, while Max stood at the shallow end recording the dog's performance. Matisse walked along the springboard on his hind legs and then stopped, poised precariously at the end. Jerry let him wobble unsteadily for a few seconds and then gave a curt command. Slowly Matisse toppled forward, executed a passable front flipover and dived head first into the water. Jerry and Carmen appalauded enthusiastically and the dog swam eagerly to the steps, clambered out, shook himself vigorously and flung a soaking spray of chlorinated water all over Barbara. But Barabara was relaxed and immersed in Mr. Vidal's prose and she barely noticed.

David came out of the kitchen eating a slice of apple pie and looking worried.

'Hey Dave, Matisse just did a dive!' Jerry cried proudly, climbing out of the pool.

David stood on the patio staring across the lawn as if he could see the writing on the wall. 'We may find ourselves with a strike down in Tiajuana,' he muttered to nobody in particular. 'Those Mexicans are driving me crazy . . . I'm nervous as hell . . . The Chinese are getting cold feet . . . It could kill us.'

'Are the Chinese still coming for New Year's Eve?' Barbara murmured, not looking up from her book.

Her husband nodded absently and munched his pie. 'Yeah, I think so Barb.'

Barbara turned the page. 'Dave, that was wonderful last night,' she whispered, putting out her hand and stroking the inside of his trouser leg.

Jerry dived into the pool with a huge splash and Matisse followed him. They swam around together like characters from a boy and dolphin saga.

David clutched his temples. 'The dog is giving me a headache,' he moaned.

Jerry turned over onto his back and Matisse jumped onto his chest. 'You sure it ain't me, Dave?' Jerry asked.

David yawned and took another large bite of pie. 'I'm not sure of anything any more,' he admitted glumly.

Jerry swam to the edge and Matisse jumped ashore, splashing water over David's shoes. 'I'm getting on your nerves Dave,' Jerry told him. 'I've outstayed my welcome here.'

David stepped back as Matisse shook water all over his suit. 'No . . . It's just that I'd like to see you making more use of your talents Jerry.'

Jerry floated lazily. 'My talent is to survive,' he said complacently.

'I could get you a wonderful job managing one of my trailer parks,' David offered, almost in desperation. 'I would be a steady thing. And clean air, by the ocean and everything.'

Jerry contemplated his toes floating some way off. 'Thanks Dave, but I don't reckon I'd be any good at that.'

'Sure you would, Jerry.'

Jerry did a few lethargic backstrokes. 'People are always complaining. Their septic tanks are overflowing . . . Their trailer is sliding down the hill . . . I don't think I could handle the responsibility, Dave.'

David stole a glance at Barbara who was still reading her book but obviously listening closely to the conversation at the same time. 'Well, I could still take you on at the hanger factory,' he suggested, as if it were a last resort.

Jerry swam over and climbed out of the pool. He took the towel Carmen brought him and smiled at everyone in turn. 'No, I really think it's time to go,' he said resolutely, starting to dry his hair.

No one spoke for a while. Barbara glanced at David. David glanced at Carmen. Carmen glanced at Barbara. They all looked at Jerry.

'At least stay . . . At least stay through the holidays . . .' David pleaded, as though his sanity depended on it.

Without the slightest hesitation Jerry threw the towel back to Carmen. 'You're the boss Dave,' he shrugged, and he dived back into the pool, drenching the others with a sheet of water.

A little later Jerry climbed out of the pool and wandered into the cabana to change. Max followed him. 'Thanks Jerry,' he said shyly, lingering in the doorway.

'For what, Max?'

The boy nodded over his shoulder towards the house. 'That was a big moment for me. When you saw me in the bathroom.'

Jerry shrugged kindly and slipped off his shorts. 'You have to be what you're going to be,' he said simply, drying himself.

Max shook his head. 'But I'm still not sure what I'm going to be Jerry,' he confessed almost naively.

'Listen Max, you can't hide for ever,' Jerry said sternly. 'Anyway, what's the big deal?'

Max hesitated. 'It's my dad really . . .'

Jerry pulled on the Terrycloth robe. 'Believe me Max, your dad's a lot more tolerant than you think. I mean look what he did for me.'

Max struggled with his uncertainty, thankful to be able to talk to someone at last. 'I'm afraid to bring my friends home,' he went on. 'I'm afraid my parents will psyche me out.'

Jerry laughed and took his arm, touched by his awkward uncertainty and his trust. 'Your mom and dad have both been around,' he said. 'Try talking to them. Really, I think you'll be surprised how much they understand.'

The boy looked doubtful for a moment and then his face relaxed and brightened. 'Okay Jerry. Okay. And thanks again.'

As Max turned to leave, Jerry pointed to his lips. 'And don't forget what I said about orange . . .' he advised. 'It'll be much more you.'

Jerry went back out on the patio and found Barbara still sitting reading alone. She asked him to massage her shoulders. Jerry looked around. David had gone to fetch his briefcase and call a cab to take him to the plant. Carmen had gone into the kitchen. They were alone. Jerry slipped Barbara's blouse down over her shoulders and began to manipulate her neck with slow skilful hands. Barbara continued reading her novel, occasionally murmuring with pleasure as he gradually increased the firmness of his touch.

'This is absolutely the last time I'll ask you to do this Jerry, I swear it is,' she vowed, squirming with satisfaction.

Out the front, David came out of the house just as the car drove up to the gates. As he strode down the driveway. Mr. Nagamichi came trotting out from under the trees carrying his hoe. 'I got to tell you Mr. Whiteman, something is killing the azaleas here and your begonias in the back . . . Killed one hydrangea too . . .' he said unhappily, doing his best to keep pace with his short legs. 'At first I thought it could be the dog was watering them, but the damage is too big for little dog. I don't want you to think it's me or my boy.'

David gritted his teeth and kept on walking. 'We both

know who's peeing on the shrubs Mr. Nagamichi,' he snapped.

The little gardener closed the gates behind his employer. 'You know Mr. Dave, you look like you could use a vacation,' he ventured, peering shrewdly through his thick lenses.

David stopped on the sidewalk with his hand on the cab door.

'I got a condo in Hawaii . . . Napilikai on Maui . . . You could use it anytime,' Mr. Nagamichi grinned toothily. 'You and wife . . . Beautiful beaches. Golf. You name it . . .'

David opened the door and got into the cab. 'Thanks,' he said, slamming the door and nodding to the driver.

Mr. Nagamichi watched the cab out of sight and then shuffled back to tend the ravaged plants.

# CHAPTER 24

Several nights later, under a waning moon and a sky filled with stars, a laughing cheering crowd was gathered on the Whitemans' patio where a strip of glowing charcoal had been laid beside the swimming pool. Barbara, Carmen, Sidney, Pearl, Lou and Max were drinking wine and finishing the remains of a gigantic pizza, while Matisse watched in awed adoration as Jerry taught everyone to walk across the hot coals. Sheila Waltzburg stood hesitant and barefoot at one end of the strip of charcoal with her eyes tightly shut and holding her glass in front of her face like a ritual chalice. The others shouted encouragement to her and slapped their thighs in slow rhythmic support.

Finally, Sheila took a fortifying swig of white wine, put her hand over her eyes and rushed along the hot smoking charcoal to be greeted at the other end by her proud husband's embrace.

'You did it Babe, you did it!' Lou yelled, grinning and exposing his flashing white teeth. The couple danced a pirouette or two in celebration and then turned to watch Barbara.

Their hostess was poised at the edge of the menacingly glowing charcoal with her eyes fixed in rapture on the moon. 'Jerry, I'm afraid . . .' she whispered, like a child facing a fresh ordeal in the playground.

Jerry stood at the other end of the strip of coals with his arms outstretched in welcome. 'Now remember Barbara, you have to concentrate on what I told you,' he said mercilessly. 'It's all in the mind.'

Barbara blushed. 'Can I go to the bathroom?' she begged. 'I'm going to wet my pants.' Her bare feet squirmed on the cold paving.

'You'll put the fire out!' Sidney chuckled, provoking a shriek of laughter all round.

Jerry raised his clenched fist above his head and punched

the air defiantly. 'Go! Go! Go! Go!' he commanded her, his eyes burning like the charcoal with almost Svengaliesque authority.

Matisse threw up his head and imitated Jerry's warcry with a staccato string of yelps.

Startled, Barbara flung her arms in the air and ran along the dreaded strip screaming and dancing like a dervish. At the other end she fell into Jerry's arms laughing hysterically.

At that precise moment, David walked round the corner from the front of the house carrying his briefcase and loosening his tie. He stopped abruptly and gaped at the wild scene in front of him.

'Dave! Dave! I just walked on fire!' Barbara shrieked ecstatically. 'I walked on fire!'

Her husband ripped off his tie and grinned weakly. 'That's great Barb, just great. My bitch of a day is made. . . .'

Not to be outdone, Carmen whipped off her shoes, hitched up her skirt and ran to the start of the fiery path. 'Watch me Dave, I am next,' she cried.

Barbara looked daggers at her maid.

'Jerry learned it in India,' Sheila told David, stuffing a wedge of pizza into her painted mouth.

'Try it, Dave!' Lou shouted from the drinks table.

'Yeah, come on honey!' Barbara insisted. 'You can do it too!'

David turned back to the house. 'Forget it,' he mumbled, crumbling with fatigue.

Lou grabbed his old friend's arm. 'Anybody in his right mind would be crazy not to do this,' he claimed.

Max ran up with his camera at the ready. 'Yes, come on Dad, try it!' he shouted.

David rounded on the noisy throng and glared at them in ill- concealed contempt. 'Some person . . .' he hissed through clenched teeth, 'some person has been pissing on my hydrangeas.'

The crowd of revellers fell silent and stared at one another in embarrassment. Then there was a sudden explosion of piercing barks and Matisse scampered along the fire walk in imitation of the humans.

'Go! Go! Go!' Jerry laughed, clapping his hands and whistling.

All except David and Carmen echoed the cheer for the plucky animal. Carmen stood waiting to show off and fuming that the hated dog had upstaged her in front of David. And David spun on his heel and strode glowering into the house.

Next door, the taper-recorded prayer summons of the *muezzin* suddenly burst into life from the unfinished minaret, drowning Matisse's yelps and the humans' applause in a cacophony of alien bleats and wails.

Several hours later, Barbara sat at her mirrors performing her nightly facial nutrition ceremony with deep concentration, while her husband slid Max's latest video epistle into the bedroom video machine and flopped onto the end of the bed to take off his gold-buckled business shoes.

Max's spikey red head appeared as usual on the screen. 'Hi Mom. Hi Dad. Jerry has urged me to try to communicate with you,' he said brightly. 'Too often in our relationshipn you've shown only anger to me. . . .'

David dropped his shoes and covered his face in his hands.

Barbara realised that he was about to get really upset and she rose and came over to him. 'There, there Baby . . .' she cooed, stroking his neck.

'Jerry says that anger will get you nowhere,' Max went on relentlessly. 'So here are some examples of your anger. . . .'

David shuddered and forced himself to look at the screen, while Barbara stood with her hands on his shoulders gazing mistily through her long eyelashes.

A rapid succession of scenes chased each other across the screen, scenes of disruption and anger showing David or Barbara shouting at Max, or at Matisse, or at each other, or at Jerry, or Orvis or at Carmen. The montage lasted about twenty seconds, but its impact was devastating. At the end Max reappeared. 'That's all I guess. P. S. I love you folks.' The picture faded to black and the tape stopped.

David sat in silent disillusionment for a moment and then glanced beseechingly up at his speechless wife. 'Okay okay but why the hell doesn't he show any of the nice times?' he whimpered, sniffing tearfully and biting at his moustache.

Barbara sighed. 'He's trying to educate us, Dave. He's trying to say something to us.'

David blew his nose and shrugged helplessly. 'Maybe we should call Dr. Toni Grant,' he suggested bitterly.

Barbara glanced sharply down at the top of his head and then moved back to finish her toilette at the dressing table.

David removed the rest of his clothes and then got into bed. 'That boy. . . . He loves Jerry more than he loves me,' he moaned.

Eventually Barbara slipped into bed beside him. 'Relax darling,' she cooed. 'You feeling . . . You feeling sexy tonight?'

Her husband closed his blue eyes and shuddered. 'No Barb, I am not feeling sexy tonight.'

She put her hand under the sheet and started to massage his chest. 'It might calm you, darling.'

But he was lost in his preoccupation with the shattered family situation. 'I've got to do something about Jerry,' he said, as if he were making a momentous discovery.

'But not tonight,' Barbara told him firmly. 'Tonight I'm going to give your aura a massage.'

'I mean, he's pissing in the yard, killing the flowers, corrupting the dog and cleaning out the refrigerator.'

'He has helped my headaches, Dave.'

'I mean, I offered the guy a job, Barb, and he told me it was too much trouble. . . .' David's voice began to rise in disbelief as he reviewed Jerry Baskins's trangresssions. 'That's it, Barb. I mean enough's enough. I've got to get him out of here.'

Barbara increased her firm *effleurage*. 'At least wait until after the New Year Party,' she murmured persuasively.

He sat up sharply and stared at her. 'How come you're defending the *schmuck*?'

Barbara nuzzled against him, 'Dave, you did a wonderful thing for that man,' she whispered. 'And you've taught me a lesson in the process. Do you see my aura, Dave?'

'And on top of all that I think he's diddling Carmen!'

There was a brief silence. Barbara snatched away her

hand with a rasping gasp of outrage. 'That bastard has to go!' she spat.

David lay back and pressed his palms over his eyes. 'I don't know about your aura, Barb, but I have a migraine . . .' he groaned, as if it were the end of the world.

# CHAPTER 25

David Whiteman's cream Rolls Royce, restored to its former gleaming splendour, swooped smoothly into the gas station forecourt and drew up at the pumps. Alone at the wheel, Jerry M. Baskins sat nodding his head in time to a rock record on the cassette stereo.

'Okay, just fill her up – Super Unleaded,' he told the attendant grandly.

At a neighbouring pump, a pretty girl in sawn off jeans and a tanktop sat at the wheel of a Toyota jeep, giving Jerry the eye as he basked in the sun through the open sliding roof. Jerry gave her a patronising nod and she accelerated away, revealing Al, the talk black vagrant from Yamato's restaurant, who was foraging among the garbage in a wastebin near the cash kiosk.

Jerry's face lit up with delight and pride. 'Hey Al! Al, over here! It's me! Jerry . . .' he shouted, waving his arms through the sunroof. 'Come on and get into the car, Al!'

The solemn-faced bum turned and stared dumbfounded at his old acquaintance. Then he grinned and loped across the forecourt like a long-armed basketball star. 'Hell Jerry, what a setup!' he boomed, clambering into the passenger seat. He offered Jerry his half-empty wine bottle.

Jerry shook his head firmly. 'Hell no, Al. I'm driving! he reminded him.

Al swigged from the bottle of indeterminate alcohol and settled himself into the luxurious cream leather seat. 'How you doin' Jerry?'

Jerry shrugged and held out a handful of tens to the attendant. 'I'm under a lot of pressure at the house,' he confessed. 'The guy is a nervous wreck. The wife is hornier than hell. The maid is a Mayan sex fiend. The son doesn't know if he's a son or a daughter and the dog is crazy.' He stared thirstily at the bottle. 'Hell, I do need a drink.'

Al handed it over and Jerry took a long swallow of the

raw concoction. 'Keep the change . . .' he waved grandly to the pump boy, and he turned the car out along Wilshire Boulevard.

Al sat upright beside him grinning like a child at the dash-board instruments, and at the puzzled glances of the passers-by and of the other drivers as they glided past.

At the beach they picked up Tom Tom, Patrick, Ed and Dorothy and then headed back up towards Beverly Hills, drinking and laughing and swinging to the throbbing stereo.

'You folks hungry?' Jerry asked.

Tom Tom nodded eagerly, 'Let's pick up a loaf of bread and some bologna,' he suggested.

But Jerry had bigger ideas, and twenty minutes later they drew up outside *Le Petit Kyoto*. A bewildered Parking Valet opened the doors and gaped as the disreputable gang tumbled out onto the sidewalk. Al and Ed glanced around them a touch furtively.

Ed stared dubiously at the trendy restaurant and its fashionable clientele. 'Hey, I don't want no trouble with the cops, Jerry,' he muttered.

Jerry gave the valet the car-keys and took Ed by the arm. 'It's okay Ed, I got plenty of dough,' he assured him, leading the way towards a large circular table vacant in the centre of the restaurant.

As the bums filed past him, a trendily dressed movie executive leaned over his female lunch companion. 'Jeez, these British rock groups are really getting sleazy,' he growled.

The girl gazed wide-eyed at the sharply attired Jerry. 'Actually Darryl, I think it's Willie Nelson,' she pouted dreamily.

Mr. Yamato eyed the approaching rabble with momentary horror, and then quickly regained his customary aplomb as he hurried to greet his guests with a slant-eyed smile of welcome. 'Mr. Baskins . . . So nice to see you again, sir. Table for . . . Table for six?'

Jerry peeled a twenty from the wad of crisp new bills Mr. Masoud had given him over the fence and handed i to the harrassed little proprietor. 'We're in a kind of a hurry Yamato,' he said.

The Japanese fussed over the bums as they seated themselves in the centre of the restaurant. 'Something to drink?' he sang, trying to ignore Al as he palmed a bread roll from a neighbouring table.

Tom Tom grimaced. 'Got any Ripple?'

Jerry frowned. 'How about some champagne cocktails all round?'

'Vodka straight up,' said Ed, boggle eyed.

'Wild Turkey,' Al ordered thirstily.

As Mr. Yamato scuttled away to fetch the drinks, Roxanne Philobosian stopped at their table on her way out. She smiled at Jerry. 'How are you, Jerry?' she purred, almost resting her tits on Patrick's head.

'Nice to see you, Roxanne,' Jerry grinned, basking in the awed admiration of his companions as he greeted the glamorous Script Consultant.

'I'm not at MGM any more,' she murmured, her sharp nipples brushing Jerry's ear, 'I'm over at Columbia now and I must say I'm *much* happier there. Don't forget to keep in touch.'

The bums nudged one another and uttered low whistles as Roxanne gave them all a cheery wave and strode majestically on her way.

An hour later, the party piled merrily out onto the sidewalk, their stomachs full of food and their bloodstreams replete with alcohol.

'That was real nice, Jerry, real nice,' Dorothy giggled, kissing him on the cheek.

'Hey, let's do it every Christmas,' he agreed.

Just then Orvis Goodnight glided up to the entrance in his cream Rolls. As he handed his keys to the valet he noticed Jerry and his friends.

'Hey Orvis!' Jerry laughed drunkenly.

The record mogul backed round them, gaping and grinning nervously. 'Oh hallo there, white man . . .' he mumbled in confusion, turning and escaping among the outdoor tables.

The Whiteman Rolls drove up and the other valet got out looking close to tears. '*Con permeso, Señor* . . . Somebody . . . Somebody have stolen the radio,' he whimpered miserably. 'It's not my fault.'

Jerry went pale. 'Oh my God,' he gasped, making no attempt to conceal his anxiety. 'Oh my God, Dave's gonna fry me for this.'

As if alerted by some secret signal, the bums immediately began to scatter. Al took off like a shot with Ed close behind him. Dorothy, Patrick and Tom Tom behaved a little more subtly and just waved and started to walk away.

'Thanks again Jerry,' Dorothy called.

The Parking Valet shook his head sadly. 'It's not safe in Beverly Hills any more,' he lamented, tearfully, handing Jerry the keys. 'It's just not safe . . .'

Jerry gazed after his departing friends, tempted to round them up and frisk them. But then he shrugged wryly, slid into the driving seat and drove away.

# CHAPTER 26

David Whiteman carried his daughter's bag down the escalator of the terminal building to the exit. Jenny walked at his side, clearly delighted to see him again.

'I thought you were bringing your boyfriend home with you, sweetheart,' he said as they exited through the automatic doors.

Jenny shoved her wadge of gum over to the other side of her mouth. 'What a wimp *he* turned out to be,' she scoffed.

'That Jim guy, honey?' Her father sounded deeply disappointed.

'Yeah, Dad. A total drug addict.' She took his arm. 'Tell me about this Jerry guy. Mother wrote me that he's very gifted.'

David forged ahead with her suitcase. 'He's okay,' he said shortly. 'Hey honey, on the way home we can stop at the deli.'

The very mention of food seemed to make Jenny feel nauseous. 'I'm getting ill already!' she protested weakly.

'But you used to love Al's. I'll walk you round there for a corned beef sandwich.'

'But I was only ten years old then,' Jenny exclaimed.

As they came out into the chilly night air Jenny saw the Rolls with Matisse on the back seat and Jerry standing at the door like a chauffeur.

David introduced them.

'You're the one who doesn't eat,' Jerry said, while David stowed her suitcase in the trunk.

'Yes, well I understand that you're quite a legend in your own time Mr. Baskins,' Jenny retorted, getting into the passenger seat.

David climbed into the driving seat and Jerry was obliged to sit in the back with Matisse.

'Oh I'm just a bum,' Jerry shrugged as they drove off.

Jenny laughed drily. 'Really? You look more like a millionaire to me.'

David laughed. 'You should see the way the guy eats,' he told her pointedly.

Jenny chewed her gum furiously and looked a little green. 'Can we have some music Dad?' she asked morosely.

Her father shook his head. 'Sorry honey, but somebody stole the Blaupunckt. I'm lucky to have a set of tyres left.'

Jerry leaned forward behind Jenny. 'There's so much dishonesty around these days,' he murmured intimately.

Jenny stiffened and stared woodenly through the windscreen at the grinning Santas along the boulevard. 'Really? I wouldn't know,' she snapped.


As soon as they reached home Jenny went straight to the kitchen to help her mother prepare dinner.

'I think I'll transfer to Vassar College, Mom,' she told Barbara as they made fruit salad together. 'It means I could do an exchange and study in Italy in the junior year.'

Barbara smiled, happy to have daughter near her again. 'Yes, I think Europe would be good for you, darling.'

Jenny was silent for a while. 'What's with this Jerry, Mom?' she said eventually. 'There's something about him I just don't trust.'

They carried the dessert into the dining room. 'He has a rare . . . a strange kind of wisdom, honey,' Barbara whispered mysteriously.

Jerry, David, Max and Carmen sat in formal silence as the dessert was set on the table. Max was wearing an earring, but to his father's relief he was not wielding the dreaded video. Max had left the gear in his bedroom and had obviously decided to try and communicate with his parents directly. Under the glass tabletop, Matisse sat quietly at the feet of his beloved Jerry.

'Hey Mom, is it okay if I invite a couple of my friends to New Year?' Max asked, as Barbara sat down and everyone started eating.

'Sure Max,' Barbara smiled.

'We could play some music, Mom. I'm forming a band.'

'You know any Chinese songs?' David piped up, without a trace of irony or condescension.

'How many Chinese are coming?' Max said, grinning at his dad.

'Ten. They travel in groups,' David told him, as if he were quoting from a cultural handbook.

Max looked interested. 'What kind of food are we having?'

'Kosher, Chinese and American,' Carmen announced.

David looked disconcerted. 'Oh, and I invited Orvis and his wife.'

Barbara looked pleased. 'That's nice, Dave.'

At the other end of the table, Jenny and Jerry were eying each other with open mistrust. Jenny was not eating a thing and she looked thinner than ever.

At last Jerry attempted to make conversation. 'You must've had a lot to eat on the plane,' he said with a smug smile.

Jenny visibly bristled with indignation. 'I don't remember talking to you,' she snapped sulkily.

Jerry kept smiling. 'Just that you kinda look as though you're starving.'

Jenny's pretty mouth curled in a savage scowl. 'Keep your brilliant insights to yourself, okay?' she retorted.

'We don't talk about it Jerry,' Barbara intervened as gently as she could.

Max suddenly came to life in public for the first time in weeks. 'But it's much better to talk about it. It's much better to get things like that out in the open,' he declared earnestly.

'Shut up, Max!' Jenny spat. She turned to Jerry with a look of undisguised contempt. 'You're just a troublemaker mister, so stay out of family business.'

David found himself getting to his feet. 'She's right Jerry. I think I've had it with you too,' he said harshly.

Jerry looked at them without giving anything away in his expression. 'I apologised about the radio, Dave.'

'It's not just the radio, Jerry.'

Jerry slowly took the napkin out of his shirt and rose to

his feet with solemn dignity. 'Okay folks, okay. Time for Jerry to get on his way. *Adios.*'

As he turned to leave the room, both Carmen and Max jumped up in horror. 'No . . . No . . . Jerry . . .!' they chorused.

Barbara also stood up. 'Dave, this can wait . . .' she declared with quiet firmness.

Very slowly, David sat down again. 'Okay, Barb. We'll discuss it after the party,' he agreed meekly.

Jerry instantly resumed his seat and gazed defiantly across at the scowling anorexic opposite him. 'Okay Dave, you're the boss around here . . .' he shrugged, enjoying Jenny's exasperated reaction with mischievous relish as he tucked into his food again.

# CHAPTER 27

That night Jenny lay awake for hours, struggling to sort out all her conflicting feelings about eating, about her parents and the situation at home, and about her future at college. After a time she became aware that somebody was playing the piano. The music was muted and distant, but eerily seductive and whoever was playing it was undeniably talented. She slipped on her robe over her naked body, crept out of her room and followed the delicate sounds to the music room at the other end of the house. The door was ajar and she pushed it open.

Jerry Baskins was sitting in his Terrycloth bathrobe at the Steinway grand playing Debussy's *Clair de Lune*, with Matisse dozing faithfully at his feet. Jenny listened in the doorway for a minute and then went over to the piano. Jerry didn't seem at all surprised to see her there.

'Debussy?' she said quietly, standing near his shoulder.

Jerry nodded, still playing but now more delicately than before.

'You play very well for a bum.'

'Fair,' he agreed. 'I haven't played much lately though.' He grinned over his shoulder. 'Hard to find a decent piano in the alleys.'

Jenny listened for a little longer. 'Just another of your many hidden talents,' she mused, admiration and sarcasm chasing one another in her voice.

Jerry completed the section he was playing and then twisted round on the stool to look at the tall stringy teenager. 'When I played the concert circuit I always opened with Debussy,' he said nonchalantly.

Backing away a pace or two, Jenny leaned on the piano and stared at the suavely smiling stranger. 'I just want you to know that I'm on to you Jerry,' she told him with unflinching candour. 'You're quite attractive in a sick sort of way. A real sociopath. Charming, talented, iconoclastic.'

She allowed herself a mild smirk. 'I'm a psychology major you know and I'm well aware of your powers.'

Jerry said nothing, but simply watched her with his habitual noncommital stare that always seemed to force others to talk.

Jenny sat on the upper keys and the resulting discordant racket clashed horribly with the memory of the Debussy earlier. 'My parents are kind, compassionate and naive people and you are just taking advantage of their kindness and their naiveté,' she told him. 'That's disgusting and I will not tolerate it.'

Jerry watched her, a thin smile playing around the corners of his mouth.

'So Jerry Baskins, you can just find some way to leave gracefully and quietly or I'll be forced to find tougher ways to deal with you.' She leaned forward and pouted threateningly. 'The game is over Jerry, as of tonight.'

Jerry smelt her warm body under the robe as she leaned over him. Suddenly he grasped her skinny shoulders and yanked her onto his lap. He gave her a long, deeply passionate kiss with expert power and sensitivity. She melted entirely in his embrace.

Under the piano, Matisse gnawed at the carpet and panted with wildly delirious excitement . . .

On the other side of the sprawling house, the light was on in Carmen's little room. The bedroom's walls were covered with large coloured posters and photographs of Fidel Castro, Che Guevara, Lenin, Mao Tse Tung, Ho Chi Min and President Ortega . . . the movie stars and pop idols having been relegated to the garbage. On the TV, a BBC Classic Serial was showing on the local PBS Station, with characters dressed in Victorian clothes parading around in earnest conversation. The sound was turned off. Carmen and David were lying side by side on top of the bedclothes, she in her skimpy *négligé* and he in his kimono, looking very un-Victorian.

'Carmen, I can't go on like this . . .' David was telling her. 'It's killing me.'

The fiery little Salvadorean flashed her eyes and drew

heavily on her cigarette. 'Oh get out. You betrayed me. Get out!' she snapped contemptuously.

David waved his hands about hopelessly. 'But Carmen, she's my *wife*,' he protested.

The maid uttered a dismissive laugh. 'Ha! I knew you would say that!' she sneered.

He tried to take her hand. 'Don't you like me, Carmen?' he murmured, edging closer to her.

Carmen snatched back her hand and blew smoke into his face. 'It is not the point Dave,' she retorted, 'even if I do think you are really cute. But now I see the big picture.'

David glanced nervously up at the political portraits on the posters around the bed. 'What big picture?' he asked in confusion.

'You are like the big imperialist,' Carmen explained, 'using me like the Third World.'

He gazed at her, totally baffled. 'What're you talking about?'

Carmen puffed at her cigarette and arranged her *négligé* a little more chastely. 'We are now in a very big struggle Dave. I am the worker and you are the capitalist.' She pointed at the posters. 'The only way to change this is the revolution. Right now!'

David shook his head in helpless bewilderment. 'But Baby, we were having such fun!'

'Yes Dave, decadent fun.'

'What happened Carmen, did you just join a communist discussion group or something?' He succeeded in taking her hand and gave her a sympathetic smile. 'My father was a communist during the Depression,' he revealed.

Carmen stopped frowning. 'Señor Mel?' she exclaimed, full of admiration. But then she scowled again. 'You are a traitor to your class!' she accused him.

'Where the hell are you learning all this stuff?'

'Books.'

'What kind of books?'

Carmen shot him a coy and evasive glance. 'Señor Jerry.'

David let go of her hand and recoiled across the narrow bed in fury and disgust. 'Jerry . . .!' he cried, a murderous glint shining in his eyes. 'That bastard . . .!'

If he hadn't been making quite so much noise, David would probably have heard the ecstatic sounds emanating from the cabana out on the patio. Inside the cramped little hut, Jenny was writhing naked on the floor while Jerry made skilful and passionate love to her. The emaciated girl threw her head from side to side, her wildly staring eyes opening and closing in time to the rhythmic thrusts of her seducer as she gyrated her pelvis in perfect harmony with his. Jerry's glistening backside flexed and relaxed in precise and ptent tempo as he surged back and forth balanced on his elbows.

Matisse lay nearby, his eyes popping out of his head as Jenny moaned and whimpered with rising and shuddering passion.

'Oh Jerry . . . Jerry . . . Jerry . . .' she panted, devouring his tongue and running her fingernails up and down his back. 'You're . . . You're, so . . . You're so *talented* . . .!'

# CHAPTER 28

The Whitemans pulled out all the stops for the New Year and their party for the Chinese Trade Delegation was a glittering occasion. The house was lavishly decorated with Chinese lanterns, paper dragons and in the entrance hall a magnificent antique gong took pride of place. There were flowers from the garden everywhere. Around the pool and the patio, coloured lights twinkled in the trees and the pool itself was a blaze of iridescent colours from spotlights fitted with old film studio gels which Jerry had found in a garbage dumpster. The Japanese miniature garden and waterfall added an exotic if not quite appropriate oriental touch. David had engaged a Chinese caterer and waiters, but there was a six-foot-six black bartender in shorts and a bowtie because of a mixup over bookings. Three Mexican musicians complete with ponchos and gigantic sombreros provided live music and a bizarre contrast to the oriental decor and cuisine.

Barbara looked quite magnificent in a long Chinese gown decorated with goldleaf and the most delicate embroidery, and she easily outshone all the other female guests as she welcomed them at the door. Mel and Sadie Whiteman, Pearl and Sidney Waxman, Geraldo, Yogi Bir, Lou and Sheila Waltzburg and other more peripheral acquaintances had all donned their finery for the great event. Carmen was the odd exception in her jungle fatigues open to the waist, but her face looked pert and saucy under the forage cap. Jenny Whiteman looked stunning, though rather insubstantial, in her loose fitting tracksuit outfit.

Lou and Sheila were ecstatic about their hostess's gown. 'The Chinese will love it. A great touch Barbara,' Lou complimented her.

David nodded anxiously but proudly in the background, dressed in his finest tuxedo and a red bowtie.

Barbara was genuinely flattered. 'Why thank you, Lou. Just wait until they see the fireworks,' she promised.

'Here they come! There's Minister Chan . . .' David suddenly exclaimed as the caterer appeared from the kitchen followed by half a dozen Chinese assistants and waiters carrying enormous salvers and bowls filled with delicious food. He had been so nervous that every time he saw an oriental face he assumed the delegation had arrived.

'Relax Dave, that's the caterer again,' Barbara murmured. 'Hey, I hope they brought enough *Abalone Delight*.' She hurried over to check, taking rapid, tiny steps in the narrow-hemmed gown.

In the cabana, Matisse sat by the door watching Jerry struggling into a Santa Claus outfit that was rather on the small side. With his rouged cheeks puffed out under the white plastic beard, Jerry looked like a Wilshire Boulevard street decoration come to life.

After a lull in the arrivals, the Mexican trio gave a fanfare and Orvis Goodnight entered in a white tuxedo with his gorgeous white wife on his arm. David greeted them warmly.

'I'd like you to meet my wife, Sandra,' Orvis boomed.

David looked suitably impressed and disarmed by the tall creature's beautiful wide smile. He introduced the splendid couple to the other guests.

'Pleasure everybody,' Orvis boomed with heavy condescension.

Barbara introduced Geraldo and Ran Bir.

'Gorgeous house,' Sandra exclaimed in her grating New York accent, ignoring Geraldo and the *yogi*.

David's mother bent her head to Mel's deaf ear. 'Is that his *wife*? The white girl?' she inquired loudly.

Mel's lugubrious features grew even gloomier. 'They don't *have* any white meat,' he complained, turning off his deaf aid.

Sidney grabbed his boss's arm. 'We're buying into a retirement home in Phoenix,' he said, nodding significantly at Orvis and Sandra.

'My business manager . . .' David explained, introducing Sidney to his neighbours.

Orvis grinned broadly. 'I just put a few pennies into a Middle East deal,' he said modestly.

Sidney's eyes lit up. 'Oil?' he inquired, ever on the alert for a tip.

'Camels!' Orvis guffawed, and wandered away to the bar.

The Chinese Trade Delegation arrived exactly on time in two enormous black limousines. Beaming and immaculate without a hair out of place and with his moustache neatly trimmed, David greeted the twelve sombrely dressed Chinese at the door, while the Mexicans played a short pastiche of oriental film music in their sombreros. The eight Chinese men and four Chinese women bowed and smiled as David shook hands and ushered them inside.

'Welcome to my home . . .' he said in loud, slow phrasing, as if the visitors were deaf as well as foreign. 'Minister Chan, Minister Dong and all the other Ministers and Managers . . . I see Mr. Lee there . . .'

The inscrutably grinning Mr. Chang said something in Chinese and the whole delegation laughed and nodded enthusiastically.

The lady translator turned to their host. 'Minister Chan says is it all right if we hang around?'

The Chinese all laughed again and looked expectantly at David. He smiled and then glanced uneasily at Barbara.

'Business joke,' said the translator, translating her translation. 'Get it? Hang around, Hangers. *Hang*?'

David grinned with relief. 'Oh yes, I get the *hang* of it,' he replied.

The lady translated his response and the delegation all threw up their hands to a person and laughed and applauded warmly.

'This is my wife, Barbara,' said David, sticking a finger into his tight collar and vainly trying to loosen it.

Barbara bowed in the Japanese style she had seen in the movies, thinking it would be acceptable to the Chinese as well. The delegation bowed and smiled and Minister Chan said a few words in Chinese.

'Brightest flower in the garden,' said the translator.

Radiant with pleasure, Barbara spread her winglike

127

sleeves in welcome. 'Would the Minister care for some *Shanghai Plum Wine*?' she purred, leading the way into the living-room.

Chinese was spoken.

'Tab with a slice of lemon please,' smiled the translator.

David introduced Jenny and then looked around for his son. 'Where's Max?' he asked Jenny, his voice betraying nervous irritation.

'He's gone to collect his friends, Dad. He'll be here in a minute.'

David explained and the translator spoke to Chan.

'One day in the future my son will manage the business,' David lied proudly.

Minister Chan nodded with approval at this evidence of stable business tradition. Then his eyes lit up as Carmen approached with drinks for everyone. Despite her jungle fatigues she looked very seductive indeed.

'*Viva la revolución*! More power to the people. I believe in Marx . . .' Carmen cried as she served the drinks.

Chan listened to the translation as he sipped his Tab and his smile instantly evaporated. He spoke rapidly in Chinese for several seconds and then gave Carmen a wink.

'Radical leftist garbage,' smiled the translator.

The delegation fell upon the sumptuous exotic buffet like vultures, busily eating and chattering among themselves and with their hosts. David caught sight of Jerry in his Santa Claus suit out in the hallway, distributing party favours to the less important guests. He hurried out and brought the merry red and white fur clad figure in to meet the Chinese.

'Please tell Minister Chan that only a few weeks ago this man was eating garbage,' David said proudly.

The translator translated and Mr. Chan stared at Jerry in astonishment. He spoke rapidly in Chinese and then sipped his *Birds' Nest Soup* with delicate gestures of the porcelain spoon.

The translator, who looked quite hungry, turned to the host. 'Why was Santa Claus eating garbage?' she asked with a mystified frown.

David laughed. 'This man is not really Santa Claus,' he

explained painstakingly. 'He is a street person who was eating garbage.'

'What is *garbage*?' asked the confused little woman.

'Garbage is trash . . . rubbish . . . things people throw away,' David replied.

The plump little lady translated this. Minister Chan nodded vigorously and shook Jerry's hand with earnest approval.

'Very efficient,' smiled the translator. 'Minister Chan says we have much to learn from the West.'

Unseen by the delegates, David grinned at Jerry and gave him a quick thumbs up signal. Jerry grinned at everyone and then started stuffing himself with delicacies from the colossal feast spread over the huge dining table. Jenny gave him a secret smile and so did Barbara and Carmen. With his red cheeks bulging with food, Jerry looked more than ever like one of the Wilshire Boulevard Santas, radiating goodwill to all people everywhere.

After the buffet, the Mexicans began to play a medley of Latin dance tunes and David and Barbara led their guests in a samba. Orvis and Sandra both picked up the beat and they soon dominated the floor despite Matisse's regular forays into the dance to snap at Orvis's heels. Then Minister Chan and Carmen burst into the dance and took over the star position, dancing superbly together as they glided rhythmically around the centre applauded by the smiling delegates.

David looked happy and relaxed, dancing cheek to cheek with Barbara. 'You're a fabulous hostess Barb,' he whispered.

She nuzzled against him. 'Let's make love tonight, Dave.'

He seized her and started a flamboyantly unorthodox pattern around the thronged room.

At that moment, Max came in with six musician friends. David immediately stopped dancing and went deathly pale. 'Oh my God . . . Oh my God . . . Oh my God . . .' he moaned, clutching Barbara like a frightened child.

Max was wearing an androgynous luminous outfit with pearls, vermilion eye-shadow and enormous earring. His

129

friends were similarly dressed, boys and girls totally indistinguishable. They were all carrying various musical instruments.

'Dad, I want you to meet some of my friends,' Max announced, his masklike face set in a grotesque smile. 'This is Billy and José, and this is Charles and Rudy and Cassy and Diane.'

The six masks nodded and leered.

'This is my band,' Max went on. 'Dad, I appreciate you're in a state of shock right now, but please don't say anything about all this until you've really thought about it, okay?'

Watched by the astounded crowd of guests who had all stopped dancing, Max kissed his father on the cheek. 'Until Jerry gave me encouragement to face the truth I was in torment, Dad.' Max glanced over at Carmen's gaping partner. 'You must be Minister Chan . . .' he called cheerily, waving his guitar. Then he noticed the red marks on David's cheek. 'Oh sorry Dad, I got some lipstick on you. Sorry.' Max wiped the marks off David's face and then led his friends out towards the patio to set up their alternative beat.

David stood among his guests grinning inanely and looking a little blue around the lips. Jerry Baskins tactfully withdrew into a corner with Matisse, having decided it was time to maintain a low profile for a while. David's mouth moved as he tried to say his son's name, but no sound came forth except for a muffled croaking.

As the dancing resumed, Jenny took his arm and steered him over to the buffet. 'Such a showoff. It's just part of growing up Dad,' she said gently. 'This kind of androgynous behaviour . . . cross dressing and everything . . . it'll soon pass.' She handed David some food. 'I mean, teenagers are under a lot of pressure . . . sexual pressure . . . and this kind of thing helps to relieve it.'

Her father nodded blankly. 'I don't know right from left any more,' he confessed, bowing and smiling at Minister Chan.

'Come on, eat!' she commanded, picking up a sweet and sour pork ball and popping it into her mouth.

David stared at her as she chewed the morsel energetically. Then his eyes brightened. 'You're . . . You're eating . . .!' he grinned. 'Darling girl you're *eating*!' He hugged her with one arm and shoved some rice into his own mouth with his free hand as if to encourage her.

'I'm starving, Dad.'

'My little angel . . .' David cried, tears welling in his blue eyes.

Jenny grasped his hand in excitement. 'You see, I'm in love, Dad. Passionately in love,' she revealed, munching passionately.

David hesitated. 'Who is it?' he asked furtively.

Jenny smiled. 'Nobody was ever good enough for me, Dad. I needed the antithesis of you because I guess nobody could ever measure up to you. And I behaved like a real bitch. I was the princess . . .' She drew closer to her father. 'But once I got rid of all my illusions and my stupid preconceptions and once I got down to some raw feelings . . . It was magic!'

David stuffed some more rice and a piece of lemon chicken into his mouth. 'So who do I have to thank for this little miracle?' he asked, chewing as though his life depended on it.

'Jerry.'

David chewed even faster. 'Jerry? Jerry who?'

'Oh Dad, *our* Jerry. Santa Claus,' Jenny laughed, choosing a large piece of Peking Duck and closing her eyes with rapture as she ate it. 'It *was* a miracle Dad. Jerry does have a kind of wisdom in him.'

David Whiteman's breathing was getting more rapid and deeper as he swallowed his mouthful. No longer pale, he was flushed and perspiring now. 'And . . . And did you . . .?' he muttered.

Jenny's face was radiant. 'Oh yes Dad, we did. We made love and it was like . . .'

David flung his plate so high that it smashed against the ceiling and showered down over him like white porcelain confetti. At the same time he uttered a primeval howl of disappointment, frustration and rage. Spinning round, he scanned the assembled guests in search of his mortal enemy.

131

In his corner, Matisse let out a startled yelp and cowered behind a chair.

Jerry was dancing vigorously with Barbara in the middle of the room. The couple paused and stared at the enraged figure standing by the buffet. Gradually the dancing stopped and everyone turned to look at David as he slowly advanced on Jerry, his mouth opening and shutting with incoherent noises. Barbara clutched Jerry's arm, her face ficed in a look of appalled anxiety.

Jerry glanced at Jenny's anguished face and sized up the situation in a flash. He detached himself from Barbara and started backing away towards the door, his rosy cheeks still inflated in merry *bonhomie*.

'You . . . took . . . my . . . baby . . .!' David suddenly exploded, in a machine-gun-like staccato. Then, like a bull from the gate bounding into the arena, he abruptly charged at Jerry.

Encumbered by the awkwardly-fitting Santa Claus outfit, Jerry turned, ran out down the hallway and out onto the patio, with David bellowing and screaming at his heels.

Barbara was white as chalk as she hitched up her long gown and attempted to run after her demented husband. Jenny overtook her mother, yelling to her father to stop. Carmen left the astonished Minister Chan gabbling excitedly to his colleagues in Chinese, and ran after the others, screaming in Spanish at the top of her voice.

Out by the pool, Max and his friends were in the middle of setting up their instruments in the atmospheric glow of the decorative lanterns and the spotlights. Suddenly Santa Claus's frantic figure bulldozed its way through them with flailing arms, knocking them and their instruments flying in all directions.

'You . . . took . . . my . . . baby . . . You bastard . . .!' David screamed, rocketing out of the house in pursuit, followed by Jenny, Carmen and the struggling Barbara in her narrow gown.

Jerry stopped and stared frantically around, unsure where to take refuge. But David cannoned full tilt into him and the two struggling figures flew across the patio in an arc and dived into the turquoise pool, sending a sheet of water over everybody else. Weighted down by the Santa suit and the boots, Jerry floundered helplessly while David jumped up on his shoulders and forced him under the surface. The water seemed to boil as the two men fought their submerged duel, David trying to drown Jerry and Jerry struggling to free himself from his crazed attacker, while around the edge Barbara, Carmen, Jenny and Max stood yelling to David to come to his senses and leave Jerry alone.

A few seconds later, all twelve members of the Chinese Trade Delegation hurried onto the patio to see what was going on. They stood watching the obscure ritual in puzzled silence, while the translator did her best to provide some kind of running commentary.

Sidney Waxman pushed his way through the specatators and quickly improvised an explanation for the important guests. 'Ladies and gentlemen, this kind of thing happens all the time in Beverly Hills,' he announced, with a plastic public relations grin on his sweating face. 'It is customary for people to jump into swimming pools at the New Year's celebration. It's a kind of a cleansing ritual . . . rebirth . . . and getting rid of all the garbage of the past . . .'

'Garbage . . .' the delegates chorused, recognising the important word in English.

Sidney looked hurt. The translator gabbled away and the delegates frowned and grinned and bowed and murmured as they struggled to comprehend the extraordinary ceremony taking place in the water.

Max soon realised that his father was not going to take any notice of the urgent pleas from the horrified onlookers. So with a swashbuckling leap, he jumped into the pool and began to try to wrestle David away from his hapless victim. Showing admirable group solidarity, Max's six friends uttered whoops of joy and jumped in after him.

With impassive solemnity, Minister Chan buttoned his jacket. His eleven colleagues followed suit. Then Mr. Chan gave a bloodcurdling oriental battlecry and leaped into the frothing water. His colleagues instantly followed their leader like lemmings over a cliff.

Orvis and his wife were next to appear on the patio, closely followed by Lou and Sheila and then Pearl searching for Sidney. Orvis seized Sandra's hand and with a booming laugh dragged her into the water after him. One by one, the remaining spectators jumped in too with shouts of inebriated recklessness. Only Sidney hung back until Pearl shoved him in and then plunged in herself.

Barking ferociously amid all the clamour, Matisse scampered out of the house and gaped at the splashing, laughing crowd of revellers in the pool. Then he saw Jerry's head suddenly break surface, his white whiskers and Santa Claus nightcap plastered flat around his terrified face. Jerry spat out a stream of water and floundered, choking and yelling for help in the midst of the dozens of preoccupied rescuers who had forgotten all about him. Then David surfaced, also yelling and flailing and immediately resumed his attack on Jerry.

Matisse yelped with dismay as he saw his beloved master being viciously assaulted. He ran round the edge of the turmoil and reaching the pool filtering plant, he leaped up at the box housing the security alarm. Powerful floodlights snapped on around the garden and the wailing sirens screamed out their banshee warning around the neighbourhood.

Up on the scaffolding around the almost completed minaret, Mr. Masoud, his son Akbar and half a dozen chadoored women gazed enviously down at the bedlam raging in and around the Whitemans' pool.

'Why were we not invited?' Mr. Masoud wondered as Carmen jumped up in the water and her breasts fell out of her uniform jacket.

Akbar stared at the maid with longing while the chadoored wives averted their gaze and giggled with shock.

Soon the police helicopter came clattering over the trees. It buzzled round and round the minaret, its powerful searchlight bathing the startled Iranians in an incadnescent glare. Mel Whiteman happened to look up and see the huddled little family group apparently suspended in mid air. Befuddled with drink and scared by the apocalyptic vision in the sky, he dropped his cigar butt onto the grass. The butt happened to fall onto the touchpaper fuse connected to an elaborate and expensive firework display set up among the trees to be set off as a grand finale to the evening's entertainment.

By now there were about forty people crowded into the pool and the helicopter's searchlight picked them out like performers at an orgy in some old fashioned epic movie.

'What a fucking party!' bellowed the pilot's voice over the loudhailer as he hovered overhead.

Still playing their bland medley of South American rhythms, the Mexican trio came out onto the patio and promptly jumped into the pool with everybody else. Only Mel and Sadie were left on dry land, gazing around them with utter incomprehension.

Next moment the firework display ignited in a dazzling blaze of coloured fire and fizzing light accompanied by deafening explosions. David and Jerry stopped fighting and stood in the pool with the others, watching the spectacular show in awed silence.

By the time the police patrol cars and the alarm company van with Lance at the wheel drove up the driveway crowded with parked cars, the fireworks had almost finished. A few sporadic crackers and the last fitful jerks of the catherine wheels died away just as the astonished cops strode onto the patio. The German Shepherd scented Matisse lurking near the cabana. With a terrifying roar it slipped its chain and tore into the cabana in pursuit of the fleeing collie.

In ten seconds, Jerry Baskins's room had been reduced to a shambles.

# CHAPTER 29

As the New Year sun rose over Beverly Hills the following morning, the coloured lights around the beaming Santa Clauses strung across the boulevards flicked off for the lwst time. In the Whitemans' pool, three sombreros floated on the surface, slowly revolving in the slightest of breezes off the Pacific. Here and there floated a shoe, a tie, a stocking, a shirt, a brassiere, a pair of undershorts, a drum and a set of white whiskers. On the patio around the pool, half a dozen figures lay wrapped in towels and blankets on lilos and loungers or just on the velvet grass, sleeping and dozing and waking to the new day and the new year. All were still wearing the remains of their party clothes. Barbara's lovely oriental gown was a crumpled ruin; David's dinner suit was torn and creased beyond recognition; Jerry still wore most of the Santa Claus gear minus the boots and the whiskers. Around them lay the debris of the firework display and of the buffet supper.

Jerry Baskins groaned and muttered himself into consciousness. Painfully he raised his head off the grass and patted Matisse who was lying across his legs. 'Happy New Year . . .' he announced to the wide clear sky.

'Wise guy . . .' David groaned hoarsely, easing himself cautiously into a sitting position on his half-collapsed lounger.

Jerry winced and massaged his neck. 'You tried to kill me!' he complained wryly.

'I was provoked,' David retorted.

Jerry rolled onto his side. 'You should never have saved me in the first place,' he grumbled.

David shrugged. 'I lent you a hand and you bit it.'

Gradually Jerry sat up and surveyed the sorry state of Max, Carmen and Jenny. 'Hell Dave, I just gave people what they were looking for,' he protested with an aggrieved expression.

There was a pause while they assessed the intensity of their respective headaches and tried to count the number of aching joints.

'And Linda Evans?' David asked eventually.

Jerry shook his head glumly.

'The sister with leukemia?'

'I don't have a sister, Dave.'

'And the *ashram*?' David persisted mercilessly.

'I drove by it once.'

'In your Rolls Royce?'

Jerry grinned like a child who's been caught stealing cookies.

'And the hot coals trick?'

Jerry shrugged. 'I don't remember, Dave. I think I picked that one up at the Iowa State Fair.'

There was another pause. Jerry ruffled Matisse's ears.

David gestured to his waking family. 'And what about us?'

Jerry laughed a short evasive laugh. '*C'est la vie*.'

David swung his legs over the edge of the tilting lounger. 'You took advantage of us all. You lied!' he said indignantly.

Jerry knelt up on the grass. 'What did you want to hear, Dave? Real heartbreak? Real sorrow?' He spat into the lawn. 'It's boring.'

'How about a little honesty?' David asked pompously.

Jerry shook his tousled head and smiled at the irony of the interrogation. 'Everything you gave had a price, Dave,' he said harshly. He got to his feet and dragged off the Santa Claus baggy red pants. 'Here's your pants Santa . . .'

David pointed to his legs. 'That's my underwear too.'

Jerry walked away into the cabana.

David stared musingly into the slightly murky water in he pool, an ironic smile slowly spreading over his face. 'You know Jerry, when I first saw you I thought there but 'or the grace of God goes Dave Whiteman.'

The undershorts sailed out of the cabana and landed at is feet.

'Your first mistake,' Jerry called out smugly.

Several socks and other items of clothing were flung out of the cabana at their rightful owner.

'You're down and out because you want to be down and out,' David continued. 'You don't have the balls to commit yourself to anything.'

Several shirts and the Terrycloth robe landed on David's lap.

'You get people to like you, and then when the going gets rough you run.'

The Santa Claus outfit flew out of the cabana and landed on the patio around him.

'I know it's a dirty filthy sewer out there . . .' David waited for the next fusillade of borrowed clothing from the cabana.

After a pause, Jerry emerged from the cabana dressed in his own ragged apparel – check pants, broken sneakers, shirt in ribbons and the torn windcheater with the flapping hood. 'It's a damn sight better than this lunatic asylum . . .' he laughed, gesturing at the wreckage of the party. 'Burglar alarms, trailer parks, coathanger factories, credit cards, dog shrinks . . .'

David sprang to his feet and immediately regretted it as his hangover caught up with his head again. 'It's called commitment *amigo*!' he shouted. 'To get to the end of the rainbow you have to walk through a whole lot of shit.'

'Well I don't need it,' Jerry retorted patronisingly.

'I know. You're free. You can eat garbage,' David spat back.

'Yeah Dave, and I can piss where I want to.'

'You could have pissed here, Jerry.'

Barbara stirred underneath her blanket. 'He did,' she sighed bitterly.

Jerry shoved his hands deep into his tattered pockets and began to walk across the lawn towards the front of the house and the driveway.

'Where the hell you going?' David demanded.

Jerry waved his hands vaguely in the air. '*Quién sabe?*'

Max peered out from under a mattress and held up his right-angled fingers as if he were focusing through viewfinder. 'Departure Scene. Take one,' he murmured sleepily.

'I'll never eat again!' Jenny cried tearfully, throwing a pillow over her face as if she intended to smother herself there and then.

Carmen got up and wrapped a blanket around her naked lower half. 'Oh Jerry, at least stay for a nice *cappucino*,' she pleaded.

Before Jerry could reply, Matisse leaped up and sped across the grass to join him.

Barbara sat up on her lilo and blew her nose raucously. 'Take him, Jerry. You're the only one he loves . . .' she cried tragically.

Jerry turned and strode off down the driveway without looking back. 'Okay, come on *amigo*,' he called, '*Vamos* . . .'

At the gates, Jerry paused and looked down at the faithful dog. 'It's our lucky day, Matisse. We can go lots of places . . . Frisco, Santa Fe, Enseñada . . .' He tickled the dog's eager ears affectionately. 'Jerry's gonna show you the ropes. The best parks to sleep in and beaches where the coconuts just flop down into the palms of your hands . . .'

Matisse's ears were upright and alert, as though he understood and liked what he was hearing.

Jerry sighed and drank in the new air. 'We can make our own schedule, Matisse. Don't owe nothin' to nobody . . .'

As they set off again down the hill they came to the Whiteman's garbage dumpster at the tradesman's gate at the end of the alleyway behind the house. Matisse stopped and barked at the huge bin.

'You hungry, boy?' Jerry chuckled, impressed by his new pal's instinctive nose for food. 'Okay, Jerry's gonna fix us up some *primo* grub. Lots of real good garbage.' He reached into the dumpster and pulled out one of the discarded cans of dogfood. Placing the can on the ground, he knelt down and prepared to eat with the dog.

But Missee merely sniffed disdainfully at the tin and wandered away barking.

Jerry tasted the stale food. It was quite disgusting.

Retching with nausea, he kicked the can against the dumpster and looked up to see what Matisse was barking at.

The entire Whiteman family plus Carmen had come down to the main gates and were standing on the sidewalk gazing tearfully after their departing guest.

Jerry gazed up the hill at the family and then down the hill towards freedom. Then he looked at Matisse. The dog was looking from Jerry to the family and then back to Jerry and waggering his tail energetically. Jerry hesitated, anxious not to lose face. Then he nodded at the dog and bent down to whisper in his ear. 'Okay *amigo*, you've convinced me,' he sighed. 'Let's go grab some of their goddam *cappucino* . . .'

As Jerry turned and headed back up the hill towards the Whiteman's gates, the family and Carmen started to cheer and wave like spectators at some sporting event. Matisse barked and wagged his tail as if he were trying to detach it from his body, and he scampered back and forth in ever-decreasing sorties as Jerry drew nearer and nearer to the gates.

When he reached the waiting family Jerry was greeted with tears and open arms as if he had been absent for a decade, and was escorted up the driveway back to the house like a returning hero.

Not long after the gates had swung to behind them, a long figure appeared round the bend trudging up the hill between the lush green hedges. He was pushing a grocery cart loaded to the brim with ragged bundles, pieces of cardboard, cans and bottles and all the usual accoutrements of the street bum. Sitting atop the heap of possessions was a small tan coloured mongrel sniffing the air eagerly, its beady little eyes ever vigilant for a morsel of food.

As they drew level with the alleyway and the Whiteman's garbage dumpster, the mongrel jumped down and stuck its snub nose into the can which Jerry and Matisse had just rejected. With a yelp of disgust, it recoiled and jumped back on the cart and the tall, emaciated hobo trudged on up the hill.

Over the high hedge surrounding the Whitemans' front garden came the sound of laughter and shouting and contented barking. The mongrel sniffed the air once more and listened intently, its ugly little ears flexing eagerly. All at once it leaped off the cart again and scampered under the gates and off up the driveway. The hobo yelled hoarsely to the dog to come back, but to no avail. Then he turned the cart and pushed it up to the gates.

They swung open quite easily . . .